The Weeping Field

The Weeping Field

mariko miyake

fishcake + tamago books

For Tetsuo and Keiko…

for rice fields at twilight,
conversations lasting into the night,
and the warmth of Matsue
that in my heart will forever burn bright.

The Weeping Field

EVEN AS A CHILD, I WAS SHINING. That light inside of me was so bright, it hummed in my ears, vibrated in my chest. My father told me that I must have swallowed the sun. I believed him then. But standing outside of his house again, I could feel that light flickering, struggling to stay lit.

"You should go see him," Naoki had said. "Even just once would be enough." At the time, I didn't say anything. It was just so unlike him, so out of the blue. How could he even ask me such a thing? That day, when he came to get me from my father's house, I didn't look back. He told me not to look back. He promised that I'd never have to see Kasumi-machi again. I couldn't understand it. Why did it matter now? Deep down, I had already made up my mind. I wouldn't do it, not even for Naoki.

But even now, it amazed me how death complicates things. After Naoki died, I couldn't stop thinking about that conversation. I couldn't stop wishing that I had told him how I felt. I should have listened to him. I should have asked him why he wanted me to go. What was so important? Now, I would never know.

I don't know what finally made me decide. Maybe deep down, I hoped that my father would have something to say to me—an explanation, an apology, something. Eight years was a long time to wait for anyone.

He seemed to be waiting too. His house was exactly as I had remembered it—old, austere, the wood slowly darkening over time. Someone had opened the shoji doors to catch the breeze, but there was no wind today. I peered inside, between the slats of the tall, wooden gate. The hydrangeas were in full bloom again—a twilight blue that seemed all too melancholy for summer.

Just then, the door to the house slid open. As I waited for him to appear, I could feel my resolve slipping. It was too soon. I wasn't ready to see him yet. I turned to leave, my eyes filling with tears.

"Forgive me, Naoki."

But just as I was about to walk away, a young woman appeared outside. With her red apron and bamboo basket, she was like something out of a fairy tale. Tall, long-limbed with black hair down to her waist, her skin was as white as bone. Her cheeks and lips blushed like an apple. And the way she moved, back and forth, snipping those melancholy blossoms, I couldn't help but be reminded of a snow crane. Her eyes twinkled when they met mine, and I slowly bowed.

She pulled off her gloves and unlocked the gate. "You must be Nami," she said. Her voice was so full of warmth, I wanted to tell her everything.

"How did you know?"

"It's your eyes," she laughed. "You have your father's eyes." She smiled at me again, but I couldn't meet her gaze. In that moment, I wanted to tell her that he wasn't my father; that my real father had died a long time ago. But I knew that wasn't true, and I couldn't lie to someone who had welcomed me with such warmth. All of a sudden, I felt her hand on my arm. It was like she sensed the storm building inside of me. She held my hand in hers and unclenched my fist.

"Please," she began, "come inside." She held the gate open for me, but I couldn't move. In my mind, I had already turned back. I was halfway down the road that led out of the valley. *How I wish Naoki were here!* He would've held my hand. He would have wiped away my tears. But no matter how hard I prayed, I knew he wasn't coming back. I looked up at the house again, to that room on the second floor. Then, I closed my umbrella and watched the gate shut behind me.

The young woman picked up her basket of hydrangeas and went inside. I hesitated. The entryway was dark and full of shadows. It didn't look welcoming at all. Even though this had been my childhood home, and I had lived here once, I felt like a stranger. I couldn't bring myself to say, "I'm home" because the fact is, this place hadn't been my home for the last eight years, and in some ways, it felt even longer.

But no matter how long I had been away, the house hadn't forgotten about me. The smell of cedar wood greeted me at the door. And without a strong summer gust to sweep it away, it permeated everything—the walls, the floors, the air. It was even beginning to weave itself through my hair. All at once, I began to feel dizzy. My dress clung to my back. I could hear my heart beating in my ears now.

I followed the young woman to a room in the back of the house. "I'll be back with some tea," she said. "Please, have a seat." But I didn't want to sit down. I was suffocating in this house. It wasn't just the smell of cedar. It was the sheer weight of memory. I shouldn't have come. Inside, I was at war with myself. I wanted to run.

But as I stood on the engawa, a kind of peace settled into my heart. As a child, the veranda had always been my haven, a world unto itself, between the inside and the outside of the house. For someone like me, who had never felt firmly planted in this world or the next, that strange landing in-between always felt like home.

Standing there now, my father's garden was almost nostalgic. Since I had been here last, the maples had climbed closer to the sky, their bright green leaves sheltering the old pine below. Hydrangeas of every color dotted the space near the cherry tree. And the branches of the willow, heavy with rain, wept over a large fishpond.

Until that moment, I hadn't realized how much I had missed that quiet. Even here, at the edge of the garden, I could hear it. I closed my eyes. My heart quickened. All at once, I wanted to run to it. I wanted to be embraced by its currents like an old friend. I felt his name fall from my lips. "Naoki." But before I could escape, the young woman returned, and as if on cue, the sound of the river faded into the background.

She set down a cup of tea and a pink wagashi shaped like a peach. The young woman waited for me to join her, but I couldn't bring myself to be in that room. If given the chance, I would have stayed on that engawa forever. I could still breathe here. I could imagine that I was somewhere else. Once inside, I was afraid the house would never let me go.

All of a sudden, the smell of peaches began to fill the room. That scent was warm and cloying, and soon, it was wrapping itself around me like a warm blanket. Before I knew it, I was sitting down across from her at a low table. I brought the cup to my mouth. I tasted the tea. With each sip, I forgot about the river. And when I placed a piece of pink wagashi in my mouth, it was as though I had needed that sweetness all along.

After I had finished, we sat there in silence. The young woman admiring the garden, while I was lost in my own thoughts. I wondered who she was. She couldn't have been more than a couple of years older than me, yet she seemed so much more worldly and good.

"Sometimes," she began. "I sit here when I want to feel bright again. Do you know what I mean, Nami?"

I glanced at the young woman, her eyes gently gazing out into the garden. I had only just met her, but it was as if she could read my mind. When I was young, there were many times when I would sit on the engawa, searching for that light inside of me. But how could she have known? What did my father tell her?

"Yes," I replied finally.

"I'm so glad that you understand." She turned to look at me then. "To live with someone who is dying can be rather depressing sometimes, don't you agree?" I nodded. "If you're not careful, it can take away all of your light, so you shouldn't let it." I met her gaze. She smiled at me warmly, as if she knew what lived in my heart.

"Do you live here?"

"Forgive me! I forgot to introduce myself." The young woman pushed away from the table and bowed, touching her forehead to the floor. "I'm Akane Nakagawa, your father's nurse. It's very nice to meet you."

"You were the one who called the inn?"

"Yes."

"Did my father ask you to call me?"

She shook her head. "I wouldn't have bothered you if your father were doing well. But over the last few months—well…to put it plainly, he's dying."

"I see."

"I thought you should know. After all, you are his daughter." I studied her face. There was no judgment. In fact, she radiated a kind of tenderness from her whole being. But I didn't know how to answer her. Yes, I was his daughter, but didn't I get to decide what that meant?

"I can understand you wanting to call me. I am his only next of kin, but—"

"He's running out of time, Nami."

"What?"

"And so are you." I looked up at her again. She had to be joking. But her face was drawn, and a furrow had appeared between her brows. I wanted to push her away, to tell her no, but there was something so sincere and good at the heart of who she was that I couldn't ignore her. A part of me wanted to believe everything she said.

"What do you mean?"

"Your father isn't doing well. It's his lungs. That's what happens to people who hold their grief inside." *What did she want from me? Did she want me to feel sorry for him?* I could feel myself turning away. I didn't want her to see that anger rising inside of me. But all those years of swallowing that pain. It was too much to bear.

"I can assure you that my father didn't have anything to cry about." I could feel my voice becoming unsteady.

"He did, Nami. Much more than you know. You know, when people hurt others, their hearts are actually crying inside. Those tears that go unshed become huge waves. Your father is carrying a whole ocean inside of his lungs. And it'll keep rising, higher and higher, until one day, he'll drown."

In that moment, I couldn't say anything. Deep down, I wanted to tell her that she was wrong. But she seemed so wise and so loving beyond her years, like she could love the whole world into being with that heart. I didn't know anyone my age who could accomplish that. I didn't know anyone who could love a monster.

For a second there, I felt almost ashamed of my hatred. After all, it had been eight years already. *Shouldn't I have just let it go? Shouldn't I have let myself move on?* But my heart was too small to let him in. "And what do you want me to do about it?"

"It would be nice if you could see him."

"Why?" I laughed. "So he can forgive me for leaving him?" I didn't care how kind of a heart she had. She didn't know my father like I did.

She looked at me gently. "It's not for him, Nami. None of this is for him. It's for you. Don't you see? You cannot save your father anymore. You can only save yourself."

All of a sudden, I burst into tears. "Don't you get it? I can't even think about saving myself right now. It's too hard! I just want my life back. I want my husband. I want that light that he gave to me every day. Since he died, I'm starved for it in the darkness!"

She handed me a handkerchief. I dabbed my eyes, but the tears kept coming. "I'm so sorry, Nami. I didn't know. You seemed too young to bear the weight of that sadness."

"At twenty, I've had more than my share."

"Yes, I see."

"It was Naoki who wanted me to see my father. He told me about a month before he died. I can't do anything for him now. I didn't even get to say goodbye. But I thought, at least I could honor his wish, even though I have no idea why he asked that of me."

Akane smiled. "Your husband saw your light. That's what attracted you to him. It's a very beautiful light that he wanted to protect more than anything. But he knew that you were carrying around this darkness, and that as long as you didn't see it, you'd never shine as brightly as you were meant to. And your husband wanted you to shine bright."

Her words cut into my heart. All of the pain of the last three months came gushing forth, and there was nothing I could do to stop it. Akane sat down next to me. She put her arm around my shoulders.

"I know," she murmured. "You've had a rough time. But don't give up. Your husband doesn't want you to give up."

Akane's voice was like a salve to my heart. I don't know how long I cried, but in time, I could breathe again. I could feel some of that life returning to my body.

"Why must I see my father now? It's not like it's going to change anything. It's not going to bring Naoki back."

"He still has power over you, Nami."

"But he's not even a part of my life anymore. He hasn't been for a long time."

"Your father still lives inside of you. That's the darkness you're carrying around. And all that resentment and hatred you're holding onto keeps him burning bright."

"But if I let go of all of that, it's like he won. He doesn't have to be accountable for anything. He can just forget what happened. Don't you see?"

"It's not that simple."

Akane's words still hung in the air, but I didn't want to listen. I closed my eyes. I let the sound of water grow loud in my ears, as if it could somehow erase what she had said. But I knew that no matter how many times I ran away, her words would always be waiting for me when I returned.

"You said that I was running out of time."

"Yes, that's correct."

"What do you mean?"

"There's something that's going to happen in the near future. I can't say what, but it'll take all of you to see it through. You will need all of your light to make it to the other side."

"The other side? I don't understand. Why are you telling me this?"

"Because you are loved, Nami, more than you know. The gods want you to live."

I didn't know what to say to her. Now, she was talking about the gods? *Didn't she know?* I had forsaken them a long time ago. They had forgotten about me.

"If I saw my father today, would that change things? Would I be able to save myself?"

"Even just once would be enough." Her words hung in the air like a favorite song. I turned to look at her, my mouth gaping.

"That's what Naoki had said to me, his exact words."

"I know."

"How did you know?"

"It's not important. What is important is that we go see your father." She stood up and moved toward the door. For someone so kind and gentle, Akane had a strong resolve. It was as if there was something pulling her forward, and she was determined to drag me along with it.

The slow patter of her house slippers echoed down the hallway and up that short flight of stairs. I followed behind, but the closer I got, the more I wanted to escape. I couldn't take it. The smell of cedar wood grew stronger and stronger until, all at once, it overwhelmed me like a wave. By the time we reached my father's room, I thought I was going to die.

Akane placed her hands on my shoulders. In an instant, the peace I had experienced earlier on the engawa flooded my body. I wanted to ask her what she had done. I wanted to marvel at her gifts, anything to keep her from sliding the door open. But she wasn't going to wait for me to be ready.

Moments later, I could make out a figure on the floor. He was lying down in the shadows, eyes closed, and a blanket pulled up to his chin. I told myself that it had to be somebody else. It couldn't be my father.

It was so quiet in the room. The only sounds I heard were the fan blowing back and forth and the slow hum of his oxygen machine. I wanted to scream. I didn't care if he were dying. I wanted to drown out his voice, that voice in my head that wouldn't go away.

"Nami! Nami!" he shouted as Naoki and I ran from the house. That day, I could hear it. There was desperation in his voice. But it was too late. By that time, I was done feeling sorry for him.

Akane motioned to a space on the floor. I slipped into the room and sat down, but not before checking to see where she was. I didn't want her to leave me alone with him. Not now. Not ever. But when I looked up, she was waiting by the door. Even now, she gazed down at him with such kindness, I couldn't compete.

Tears began to well up in my eyes. I told myself that I wouldn't cry, that my father didn't deserve my tears, but I couldn't help myself. I didn't recognize him. The man before me looked so old. His face was sunken in, and his body had already shrunk down to a corpse. Akane said that he was nearing the end; that he had already arrived at that place where there was nothing, neither she nor I, could really do for him. It was too late, wasn't it? I didn't know what he could possibly give me in this moment.

Then, all of a sudden, I felt something latch onto my arm. I looked down. My father had reached out and grabbed my wrist. And no matter how hard Akane tried to pry him off of me, he wouldn't let go. His eyes flashed open. If I hadn't recognized him before, there was no question who he was now. I could never forget those eyes and the way they looked at me with such hatred.

With his other hand, my father pulled off his oxygen mask, all the while, keeping those cold eyes on mine. I steeled myself. I refused to look away, even though my hands were shaking, and there were tears running down my cheeks. No, I told myself. I wasn't going to let him win. Not this time.

He moved closer. Akane tried to pull him back, but he pushed her away.

"See what you've done," he growled. "You've broken this man." He squeezed my wrist harder. He was pressing so hard, it felt like my bones would shatter. But I swallowed that pain. I wasn't going to let him see my fear.

After Akane finally managed to pull us apart, my father lunged at me.

"It's all your fault, Sanae! Don't think you'll get away this time." At the sound of her name, my body went cold.

"I'm not Sanae! Can't you see me? I'm Nami!" But he wouldn't believe me. He began to cough and gasp for air, but I didn't care anymore. Nothing had changed, and nothing was going to. It was a mistake to even come here today. I knew that now.

In an instant, I was running, out of his room, out of his house, out of his life. Once outside the front gate, I didn't look back.

"Sanae! Sanae!" I heard him calling out after me. But I wasn't going to stop. I kept running, until I couldn't hear his voice any longer, until all I could hear was the river.

THE SOUND OF WATER WAS EVERYWHERE. I couldn't escape it. Before I knew it, I had abandoned the way home, and soon, found myself deep in the forest. The wind began to pick up. I could hear it traveling through the trees, their leaves rustling above me. I quickened my pace. I couldn't help myself. Inside, I was a child again, darting between the cedars, through that dappled sunlight on the forest floor. The sound of water grew louder. My heart pounded in my chest. Even after all this time, I hadn't forgotten the way there.

All at once, the forest ended, and the river stretched out before me like a glorious blue snake. I could hardly breathe. I stood there at the edge of the water, its surface shimmering in the afternoon light. In that moment, I didn't want to go back, not to my father's house, nor to my home in Kyoto City. All I wanted was to pretend that this was some kind of dream, that I would wake up, sooner or later, and Naoki would be right there waiting for me.

I closed my eyes. I let the sun warm my face. In my mind, I was twelve again, and I was standing at the edge of this same river.

That day, the water was so loud, I could think of nothing else. I had already made up my mind. No one was going to stop me. Not this time. But his voice cut through all the noise.

"Don't," he said to me.

I turned to look at him. He stood a couple of yards behind me, this boy with bright eyes. At the time, he was a stranger to me. I didn't know where he was from or even that he went to my school. But he stared long and hard into my eyes, as if that would make a difference.

Those eyes didn't mean anything to me back then. By that time, I didn't care that there was someone waiting for me at the shoreline. I wanted him to go away. He had no right to tell me what to do. He didn't know my story.

I stepped into the current. In an instant, the river swept me into its embrace. I didn't fight it. I let it pull me under. I let its voice lull me into a dream. And then, everything fell silent. It was exactly how I had imagined it.

He should have left me at the bottom of that river. I should have drowned that day. But he dove in. He searched the currents until he held me in his arms like a precious treasure. When I realized that he was trying to save me, I fought him. I used every ounce of strength I had left to die in that river. But he was far too determined for me. That day, even the river was no match for him.

We didn't talk or say anything afterwards. But before he let me go, he held me by the shoulders and looked hard into my eyes.

"I want you to live, no matter what," he said to me. I was so choked up that I couldn't even manage a yes. In that moment, all I could do was nod, and he smiled. "Promise me," he said. He held out his pinkie. I reached out and linked my finger with his.

"I promise."

That day, he knew nothing about me. I was just a stranger to him, yet he held me in his arms as if he knew me, as if I were someone worthy of being saved.

But Naoki couldn't save me from everything.

The river gleamed in the afternoon light. I stood there at the edge, letting its brightness blind me. I didn't want to see the darkness inside. I didn't want to go back to that time, ever. I slipped off my shoes and dropped my bag down beside me. The sound of water was so loud now, I couldn't hear anything else. I wasn't thinking anymore. I didn't care who I was leaving behind. I didn't care who I was going to hurt. All I knew was, that the person I loved most in this world had already gone on ahead of me, and I just wanted to catch up. I just wanted to be with him again. *Was that so wrong?*

The river warned me one last time, but I wasn't going to listen. I inched closer. The water was washing over my feet now. It was cold, even for summer, and that iciness ran through my veins, racing toward my heart. The river began to lap at the hem of my dress, pulling me in. My heart pounded in my ears. The world began to spin.

"Forgive me, Naoki."

But just as I was about to step down into the deep and let the current pull me under, I heard her voice. It pierced the silence of the valley; it cut through the sound of water. I froze. My heart was racing. The river kept beckoning me to come, to rest my weary body in its arms. I kept telling myself, she was only a dream. She had to be.

"Mama!" she cried out again. But she wasn't.

- 3 -

IT BEGAN TO RAIN, LIGHT GENTLE DROPS and then an all-out downpour. As the clouds gathered in the late afternoon sky, my eyes frantically searched the valley. I didn't want to believe it. Yet, I knew what I had heard. I slowly backed away from the water. The river continued to rush before me, but I had already lost my nerve.

How easy it had been to leave her behind, to run into the river's embrace, to forsake everything, to see Naoki again! Until today, I hadn't realized how much I was breaking under the weight of my grief. My daughter's own imprint, proof that I had carried her inside of me, was still alive in my womb. But even now, there was no room for her in my heart.

Since Naoki died, she hasn't smiled. She hasn't laughed, not even once. And the thing is, as her mother, I haven't done one thing about it. My daughter is still living! She's right there in front of me, but most days, I can't even see her. And I hate myself for feeling this way. But some days, I don't want to see her. She reminds me too much of all that I have lost. And her eyes. They're his.

Still, she called out to me. Her small voice cut through the sound of water. She was pleading with me to stay, begging me to live. My heart was breaking in the wake of his absence, the river of tears still flowing inside of me. But when she called out to me, I had no choice. I had to keep my feet firmly planted in this world. I should have been grateful. After all, my daughter had just saved me, but I knew that I didn't deserve it.

The stars had come out, and a sliver of a moon hung low in the sky, by the time I got back to Kyoto City. It was raining again, but it didn't matter. I told myself that I needed to hurry. I needed to see my daughter with my own eyes. But returning home now felt like crossing a river, the air so thick with grief, I just couldn't get across.

That night eight years ago, it had also been raining. We were drenched, Naoki and I, like a couple of strays, but neither one of us had noticed the rain by then. By that time,

I didn't even have to ask. One look at his face, and I knew that he was hurt; that the rage and grief were beginning to eat away at his heart. When we finally got to the inn, he dragged me inside. I tried to pull away one last time, but he wouldn't let me go.

His grandmother was waiting for us in the lobby. When she saw me standing there, drenched to the bone, I couldn't even imagine what was going on in her head. If I had been stronger then, I would have broken free. I would have run back to the river where I belonged. The last thing I wanted to do was get him involved, let alone his family. But knowing Naoki, he wouldn't have listened.

"What happened?" his grandmother asked. "You're soaked through."

She motioned to one of her staff, and the man quickly disappeared. He was going to call the police. I was sure of it. I tried to break away from Naoki again, but he wouldn't let go.

"Bachan—" I could feel it. I could feel how close his grief was to the surface. It was in the way his voice quivered, how he could barely get the words out.

"What is it, Naoki? Tell me."

"Bachan, she has to live here. Nami has to live here, with us. There's no other way."

"Naoki."

"Bachan, please." There were tears in his eyes now.

He bowed low to her. If he wasn't holding my hand, he probably would have gotten down on his hands and knees and begged her to let me stay. Deep down, I felt so ashamed. Not once in my own life, had I ever fought for myself so fiercely.

Naoki's grandmother didn't answer right away. In that moment, she was quiet, her gaze cast down to the floor, as if she were considering her options. I shut my eyes tight. I didn't want to see it. I didn't want to see her refuse me. After all that had happened, I didn't think that I could take it. All I wanted was a little warmth tonight. She didn't even have to feed me. And the next day, she wouldn't have to worry. I'd be gone.

But all at once, I felt hands on my cheeks, cupping my face as if I were this precious person. I opened my eyes. "Well, of course, she'll live here with us," she said. The man returned with a stack of towels. She took one from him and began to gently dry my hair. Tears sprung to my eyes. I had never met anyone other than Naoki, who had loved me before they even had a reason. "Oh, you'll be all right, my dear. You'll be all right."

To the day he died, Naoki never told her what had really happened. But it didn't matter. It was like she had a sixth sense about these things. I don't know why she took me in that night. I was going to be a burden on her for sure. But she never made me feel that way.

And it was Bachan who was standing outside when I turned the corner. She held a towel in her hand, just like that night eight years ago. When she saw me, she smiled and ran out to greet me.

"Welcome home, Nami."

"I'm home," I told her, and I meant it. She slipped her arm into mine, and we walked back to the inn together. When we reached the entrance, she stood there under the eaves and carefully dried my hair. I wanted to cry so badly. Her love was boundless. There were many times when I felt so unworthy of it, but she never wavered.

But those good feelings only lasted a second. When I went inside and saw my daughter curled up in the lobby, that guilt and shame choked everything good Bachan had given me. From where I stood, I couldn't get over how small Suzu looked, how fragile. In a few months, she was going to be five, but seeing her sleeping there, it was like looking at a two-year-old. *How had I missed that?*

"Nami-chan, hurry and go see your daughter. You know she won't go to bed unless she knows you're here."

"I'm so sorry, Bachan. I keep making trouble for you. I was gone so long, and you're so busy." I started to cry.

"Oh, Nami!" she cried. "You have never made trouble for me, ever. Suzu-chan and I had so much fun today."

"But I should have come back sooner."

"Nonsense!" She took my hand and led me over to the couch. But when I finally saw my daughter, I hesitated.

"Bachan."

"Go ahead." But a part of me didn't want to wake her. She looked peaceful, dreaming, softly murmuring to herself. I didn't want to disturb her. I felt tears fill my eyes. Bachan knelt down and wiped them away. "You don't want Suzu to see you like this, do you?" I shook my head.

I reached out and gently touched my daughter's arm. "Suzu?" After a few moments, she stirred and slowly opened her eyes. No matter how many times it happened, I never got used to the way she looked at me. It was like Naoki was still here. She looked so much like him now that it took all of me to smile. But she didn't smile back.

She continued to stare at me as if she didn't know who I was, as if she knew what I had done. I wanted to look away, but I couldn't. Her eyes bore into me, all the way to my heart. "Suzu-chan. It's Mama."

"Mama? Mama." She began to cry. My heart hurt so badly. It was like being at the edge of the river again. I picked her up and held her in my arms.

"I'm here, Suzu. Mama is here."

"Where did you go?"

"I just had to take care of something. You don't have to worry. I'm back now, for good."

"But you were gone for so long. I thought you weren't coming home." I couldn't even look at her. I couldn't lie to those eyes.

"No, Suzu. I'll always come back. Always," I told her. But I didn't know who I was trying to convince, my daughter or myself. She pulled away from me, her small hand touching my cheek, the furrow between her brows growing deeper.

"Promise?" she said finally.

"I promise." In that moment, I held her to me tight. I didn't want her to see my tears. I didn't want her to know that I had lied.

- 4 -

MAYBE MY DAUGHTER WOULD HAVE SUFFERED LESS if she had been born to a different mother, one who came from a good family, one who didn't have any secrets. But Suzu was unlucky in that way. She became a fox daughter without ever knowing it. I thought that once I moved in, once I became a part of Naoki's family, I'd be reborn. I'd be different, better. But no matter how hard I tried, the past just couldn't be swept away.

Not long after Naoki had died, Bachan and I met a former guest at a bakery. Her name was Fukuda, and she was an energetic spinster from the outskirts of Kyoto. I had met her before at the inn, but it had always been with Naoki. Maybe that's why I never noticed how she looked at me. I never noticed how she stared at my face and the face of my child. But that day, after Naoki had died, I felt it. It was like she was seeing me for the first time.

"I'm so sorry for your loss," she said to Bachan. Fukuda didn't need to say any more. After all, Naoki was Bachan's grandson. That, in and of itself, was a horrible loss. I didn't need any more of her sympathy. But she made it a point to move past Bachan and greet me personally.

"It's good to see you again," I told her. I kept my head down. I didn't want to look at her. I didn't want her pity. But I could feel her eyes on me.

"Naoki was such a good person," she said to me finally. "He didn't deserve to die so soon."

"Yes."

"Who knows what he would have become if he had had more time? I guess now, we'll never know." I was on the verge of tears. All I wanted was for Naoki to come through that door and tell her that this was all a terrible mistake. But I knew he wouldn't.

"Thank you for your kind words," I said to her, trying to leave. I just wanted to go home. I wanted to be alone with my grief, not here having polite conversation. I still couldn't believe he was gone. *Couldn't she see that?*

But Fukuda continued. "Even for that short while, you had love," she said to me. "You should feel so grateful,

Nami. Not everyone in your position can be so lucky." I looked up at her then. Perhaps, deep down, she had meant well, but I didn't like the tone of her voice, or the way she looked at me. I knew that look. She didn't think someone like me deserved Naoki, that I was lucky to have had eight years, that I was greedy to want more. But the longer she talked, the more I realized that it was more than that.

I took Suzu by the hand and moved her away. I didn't want her to be caught in the old woman's venom. But Fukuda wouldn't let up. She turned to Bachan then, and leaned in as if she were sharing a secret, but I could hear her perfectly. "You must know about the foxes," she said. "They say, if you see one, run away, even in your dreams."

"What are you trying to say?" Bachan asked her.

"Maybe Naoki should have run away." Before Bachan could respond, Fukuda excused herself and left the bakery.

Her words stung. In her voice, I heard the girl in my grade school class. *Fox daughter*, she had said to me. As soon as those words left her mouth, I pushed her down. I had heard much worse from the other kids in Kasumi-machi, but that day, she was just unlucky. I couldn't take it anymore. There was no room inside of me to shove down one more insult.

When the teacher pulled me off of her, I couldn't tell if I were being scolded or comforted. It had been so long since an adult had been on my side. I didn't trust them anymore. I clenched my fists. I could feel the anger burning inside of me.

Before she could say any more, I broke free and ran. I could hear her calling after me, but I wasn't going to stop. If she were a good enough teacher, she would at least pray that I would come back. But by that time, the sound of water was in my ears, and I wasn't going to stop until I got to the river.

When I reached the edge of the water, I heard the current roar before me. I loved that sound. I loved the way it felt in my body, even as a child. But I was too young. I wasn't strong enough yet. That day, I stepped back. I walked away. Eventually, I returned to school, but the sound of water had already taken hold in my heart. And it wasn't going to let go.

I was older now. I knew better. But it didn't mean that those things didn't hurt me anymore. I knew that Fukuda was talking about me. She knew something about that time before. In her mind, I was a clever fox, one who had fooled Naoki, one who by my very presence in his life was the reason he died. Had he married a different girl, from a different family, he would still be alive. Instead, my husband paid such a big price to fall in love with me. What she wanted me to know was that I couldn't fool her. Fukuda knew who I really was.

"Don't listen to her, Nami," Bachan said to me. "That old bat is just bitter, because no one wanted to marry her." I wanted to believe her, but I knew better.

In the quiet of our room, I could still hear the rush of the river. It filled my heart just as it did earlier in the day, but I no longer wanted to run to it. *How could I?* I couldn't bear to see that look on my daughter's face again, knowing what I had done, how reckless I had become. Even now, I didn't think that she would ever forgive me.

"Nami-chan? Nami-chan?" I quickly wiped away my tears. I didn't want her to see me like this. I didn't want her to worry.

"Yes?"

"Can I come in?"

"It's okay." She entered the room and sat down near the door.

"How are you doing?" she asked me.

"Okay, I guess."

This is the kind of person Bachan is. She should have been with her guests. After all, she was the proprietress of this inn. They were expecting to see her. But she was here, with me, because she knew how much I needed her.

"How's Suzu?"

I felt the steady rise and fall of my daughter's chest. "She went right back to sleep."

She didn't say anything more, and in that quiet, the sound of my daughter's breathing began to fill the room. Even now, I wondered how she could have been in the valley today, how I could have heard her voice. There was no mistake. It was her. Yet, when I held her in my arms, or saw her sleeping before me, it was very clear that she was anchored here at the inn; that she never left. My head was spinning.

"Nami-chan, listen to me. You know you didn't have to go see him, right?"

"I know."

"Naoki would have understood. If you didn't want to, he wasn't the kind of person to judge anyone, especially you. You know that, right?"

"I know. But I had to do something. When he died, I couldn't do anything for him. He did so much for me in those eight years, and all I ever did was make trouble for him."

"Oh, Nami. Come here." I buried my face in her lap. She patted my head and wiped the tears from my cheeks. "I don't think you even realize how much Naoki loved you and how grateful he was that you came into his life."

"I do, Bachan. I know he loved me."

"That day he met you at the river, it was like something inside of him woke up. You know, both his parents were gone by then, and all he had was this old lady."

"Bachan."

"You were so much more than just a cure for his loneliness, Nami. You made his heart come alive again. You gave him something to live for. He loved you so much."

"Then why didn't he stay with me? Didn't he want to be here, with us?"

"Oh, Nami."

"I miss him, Bachan. How can I go on without him?"

"I miss him too. Every morning, I still tell myself, 'Oh, I need to go wake him up!' And then, I realize that there's no longer a need."

"Is it ever going to get easier?" In that moment, I wanted her to tell me that it would, that one day, I wouldn't hurt like this anymore.

"I don't know, Nami," she said finally. "It's been three months already, but it still feels like it happened yesterday." Hot tears burned my cheeks. The room became a blur. By that time, I was crying so hard, I couldn't speak.

"Bachan."

"I know. My heart hurts too. But Naoki was a special one. Your heart is always going to hurt, even just a little."

We didn't say anything for a long time. In that silence, I heard my daughter. She was murmuring again. "Papa," she said. But I didn't want to look at her. Even sleeping, even in the shadows, she looked like Naoki. I turned my head and shut my eyes.

"Did your father have anything to say?" Bachan's voice brought me back into the room again.

"About Naoki?"

"Yes. Did he know anything?"

"I didn't even get the chance to ask him." I wanted to tell her that he wouldn't let me, that he wasn't interested. All he cared about was himself. Even now, I could still feel that throbbing in my wrist, like he was never going to let me go.

"How is he?"

"My father?"

"Yes."

"He's dying. At least that's what his nurse said."

"Oh, I see. I'm so sorry, Nami."

"Don't be." I wasn't. I could still hear him calling after me, "Sanae! Sanae!" He was never going to change. In his eyes, I'd always be my mother.

"Still, it must be hard."

"He looked pretty bad," I lied. But even now, I thought he would live forever. I could still see that expression on his face—that look of disdain, directed at me, felt immortal for sure.

"He's running out of time then," she said.

"I guess, and according to his nurse, so am I."

"You? What did she mean by that?"

I sat up and looked into her eyes. "I don't know. But I'm afraid something will happen to me, and Suzu will be left alone."

She grabbed me by the arms. "Don't think like that! I can't lose you too."

"I can't help it, Bachan."

"You and Suzu are the most precious things in my life. If you were gone, I don't know what I'd do. And what about Suzu? Hasn't she been through enough already?"

"I know."

"It's because of you, Nami, that I still want to live each day. I want to see what more you will do with your life, what fascinating person Suzu will become." I was crying again.

"Oh, Bachan." *Didn't she know?* She said I was her reason for living, but it was really the other way around. If she hadn't taken me in that night, I don't know what I would have done. I had no one else.

I looked into her eyes. "What is it, Nami?"

"Bachan, I've always wanted to know something, but I never had the courage to ask you. If my time is really running out, then I want to know the truth before it's too late."

"Don't talk like that, Nami."

"I can't help it. I don't know what's going to happen, and I don't want to leave this earth without knowing."

"What is it? I'll tell you anything."

"That night, eight years ago, why did you take me in? Why didn't you just send me away?"

"Oh, I couldn't send you away. It was obvious that you were in some kind of trouble. I had never seen Naoki so mad in my life. And if he was that angry, then I knew that he was already in love with you."

"Is that the whole answer?"

"Of course, I was selfish too. I had always wanted a granddaughter and someone for Naoki, so he wouldn't be all alone. But the truth is, you reminded me of someone I knew a long long time ago. In fact, the resemblance is uncanny."

"I look like her?"

"Yes. When Naoki brought you here that night, I had to blink my eyes and look twice. You looked so much like her, even today."

"What happened to her?" Bachan grew quiet and dabbed her eyes with her handkerchief.

"She died."

"Oh, Bachan, I'm so sorry."

"Don't be. I don't deserve your sympathy. It was my fault that she died. If I had just minded my own business, she would still be here. She would still be alive."

"Is that why you took me in?"

"Yes. The truth is, I felt guilty all these years. After she died, everyone blamed me for her death. I couldn't live with myself there. So, I left and came here to Kyoto City. But that feeling of shame never went away."

"But it happened so long ago."

"I know. But when you came here that night, looking so much like her, I felt like I had this second chance. I was going to make things right, whoever you were."

"I'm sure your friend wouldn't have blamed you, even now."

"I know, but it doesn't feel that way. I don't know if she can ever forgive me. I don't know if I can forgive myself. But, if in her own special way, she's guiding me back to her, it would fill my heart with such peace. Maybe that's the reason why I took you in."

"I hope you never regret it, Bachan."

"Never." She cupped my face in her hands like she did on that rainy night so many years ago. Her eyes were wet with tears, but she was smiling. "You're my world, Nami. You and Suzu. So, stop this nonsense talk and get some rest."

She stood up and let herself out, but her love lingered in the room. Deep down, I felt so lucky that she had taken me in that night. I felt so lucky that her friend was still alive in her heart all these years later. That memory saved me. Had she not been there, what would have happened? Where would I have gone?

I lay down next to Suzu. She was already so far away, running toward her dreams. My daughter was so trusting of the night. There was no question that she would see the dawn. I envied that kind of faith. I couldn't even remember the last time I had slept like that. Not since Naoki died, or maybe even longer. I wanted to be there with her. I wanted to let go. But I was still here at the beginning, fending off the darkness. And even with Suzu beside me, I didn't feel brave.

- 5 -

THE STREET IN FRONT OF THE INN WAS SHINY, glittering with light, but I knew it wasn't real. From my window, I saw Naoki leave. He was wearing the same clothes they found him in—that white t-shirt with the elephant on it, those dark jeans.

"Naoki! Naoki!" I called to him again and again, but he didn't look back. He didn't even try. In my heart, I was willing him not to go. I was begging him to stay. I would have gotten down on my hands and knees if he would just turn around and look at me. But by the time I got downstairs and ran out into the street, he was gone.

He had left me a thousand times in my dreams, but I never stopped hoping that this time would be different, that this time he would turn back, that maybe, just maybe, he would stay here with me. Sometimes, when I would wake in the middle of the night, I would hear him breathing again, that easy rhythm of sleep. And I would pray, deep in my heart that it was true, that he was just returning home to me from his dreams.

Maybe I was just torturing myself, but I couldn't help it. I missed him so much. I got up and pushed the curtain aside. My eyes searched the street below. It had been raining. The pavement gleamed in the pale moonlight. But there was no sign of him anywhere.

No one ever tells you when you fall in love, when you marry and have a child together, that it'll end one day. Maybe I knew this deep down. Maybe I knew that I would lose him sooner rather than later. Maybe that was all someone like me could expect. *I was lucky, wasn't I?* Eight years was a long time. But that didn't stop me from hoping it would be forever.

The day Naoki died, I wasn't even in Kyoto. Suzu and I had gone to Matsue to visit a friend, who had just opened her own confectionary shop. We were happy then. I can still picture my daughter on the train. She held a box of sweets tightly in her arms. Every now and then, she would peek inside, her eyes full of delight. She couldn't wait to give it to Naoki.

But I should have been more vigilant. I should have protected my happiness as if it were a rare treasure. If I had known that it would be the last time I would see Suzu smile, the last time I would hear her laugh, I would have cherished it more, imprinted that sound in my heart. But even now, I wondered if I had a right to be happy at all. While we were enjoying ourselves, Naoki was probably fighting for his life. There's not a day that goes by that I don't tell myself, *if only I had stayed in Kyoto, if only I had just been here, maybe he would still be alive.*

That's the thing about that day. No one knows what really happened, except maybe the gods, but they weren't talking. All we knew was, the night before, Naoki had gone to meet someone. He didn't tell Bachan who or where, just that it was important. But he never returned.

Early the next morning, they found his body floating in the river downstream from Kasumi-machi. The policeman said that he probably died on the bridge. There were no signs of a struggle. Yet he drowned. How could that be? My love, who saved me from this same river, died in its waters. They told us that it might have been a suicide, but I refused to believe it. *We were happy, weren't we?*

When Bachan came to meet us at the train station, I knew something was wrong.

"Where's Naoki?" I asked her. She smiled weakly, but she didn't say a word. Once outside, she guided us to a black sedan, where a young police detective was waiting for us.

"I'm Kataoka. I'm very sorry for your loss." I turned to Bachan, searching for an explanation, but she wouldn't even look at me. I knew. In that moment, I knew he was gone. But I didn't want to believe it. I still wanted to hold out hope that this was all a terrible mistake, that they had found the wrong man, that Naoki was just on his way home to me.

It was only when I saw his body lying there in the cold morgue that reality sank in, and that light that he had nurtured all these years began to drain from my body.

"Naoki!" I cried out. I threw myself onto his chest. He was so cold. Even if I tried to warm him up with my body, he wouldn't wake up. I wouldn't believe it. He couldn't be gone. He just couldn't. Bachan gently touched my shoulder, but I wouldn't leave him, not until I felt his arms wrap themselves around me, until I heard his voice telling me that this was just a bad dream.

But no matter how long I waited, he just wouldn't come back. In the end, all I was left with was a bag of his personal effects—his wallet, a set of keys, and his watch. How was I to explain this to a four-year-old when I couldn't even make sense of it myself?

Even now, I don't understand it. Three months have passed, and I have more questions than answers. To this day, I still can't make sense of that expression on his face. It was so serene as if his heart was at peace, as if he had gone willingly as I had wanted to years before. I felt envious of that peace. Now, I would never have it.

"Papa," she murmured. Her small voice filled up the empty silence of the room. She was dreaming again. Even in her dreams, she was calling me back, this anchor in the sea of my grief. I lay down next to her and watched her sleep. *How careless I had been!* Naoki had given me such a precious gift, and in a heartbeat, I thought nothing of throwing it away. I didn't think that he could ever forgive me now.

This is how it had always been. I had always thought only of myself. When I found out that I was pregnant, that I was going to be a mother at sixteen, I didn't tell him. I could trust Naoki. He knew me. He knew my heart. He had traveled the road to the center of my world many times before. But I didn't tell him. Maybe that was the thing about love. When someone loved you, you would rather die than disappoint them, ever.

That morning, I remember watching him leave. From my bedroom window, I saw him walking further and further away from me like he was disappearing from my life. Then, he turned the corner, and he was gone. He didn't look back. Not even once. His eyes were fixed ahead, as if I had already become a memory.

I couldn't blame him. I had already made a mess of things at breakfast. No matter how hard I tried, I couldn't hide the fact that I was pregnant. That morning, the chawan rice bowl had slipped out of my hand and cracked into angry pieces on the floor. For a second there, I turned to him. He must have seen the fear in my eyes, because he stood up. But I ran from him.

"Nami!"

In no time, I locked myself in my room, throwing up my breakfast in the toilet. And no matter how many times he called my name, I wouldn't answer.

He didn't come home until later that night. Deep down, I wanted to talk to him. I wanted to tell him that I was sorry. But by that time, I was just so ashamed. I didn't want to make more trouble for him. I didn't want him to have to carry yet one more burden.

I waited for him in the darkness. But he didn't try to talk to me. He didn't even come to my room. Instead, he went to his own room and shut the door. It didn't matter. I told myself that it was better this way. By that time, I had already made up my mind.

Midnight came and went. I hesitated, and put my bag away several times. But around two o'clock, the inn became completely silent. In that darkness, my head cleared, and I knew what I had to do. I grabbed my bag and slipped out of my room. For just a moment, I lingered outside his door. In my heart, I said everything I had wanted to say. I hoped that he felt it. I hoped that he would understand.

I turned to leave. I was careful going down the stairs. It was something I had learned a long time ago. Sometimes, being invisible was the only way to save yourself. Once at the bottom, I made my way to the back door. But I was too late.

"Don't," he whispered. His voice cut straight through to my heart.

Naoki stood there in the shadows, silently watching me. All at once, I felt so guilty. I tried to explain, but he didn't say a word. Instead, he grabbed my bag, took my hand in his, and before long, we were back in my room.

When he sat down and faced me, I couldn't even look at him. He had the same look that my daughter had today. He was hurt. He was wondering why I didn't say anything, why I just wanted to leave. I didn't say a word. I knew that there was nothing I could say or do to justify what I had done. In that moment, I wanted the ground to open up and swallow me whole.

"What's going on?" he asked me finally. He glanced at my bag in the corner of the room. "Why the bag? What were you planning on doing?" I knew that he knew the answers to those questions, but he wanted to hear it from me. He wanted me to tell him to his face that I was leaving for good, that I didn't love him.

"We shouldn't have done it," I blurted out. From the expression on his face, I knew that wasn't what he had wanted to hear. My words were like a gale wind pressing against his heart. He knew that I was trying to push him away. I wanted him to let me go. But Naoki was too smart for me. He wasn't going to fall for that.

"Do you really believe that?" He touched my face, took my hands in his. He leaned in, and his lips found mine. I could feel myself giving in to him, my lips yielding to his. I wanted him with all my being, but I forced myself to pull away.

He touched my face again. "Nami, how long have you known?"

"You knew?"

"It was hard to ignore what happened at breakfast. I knew something was wrong, but I didn't know what. It was Bachan who told me."

"Oh."

"Why didn't you tell me?" he whispered. I could feel my face grow hot with shame.

"Because I've made too much trouble for you already. It's my problem. I don't want you to have to change your life. I don't want to be a burden. You don't deserve that."

"You sound like you got pregnant all by yourself." I met his gaze, thinking he was joking. But he was dead serious.

"Of course not."

"If I remember correctly, I was right there with you."

"I know."

"If you know, then why do you think it's just your problem. There were two of us."

"I don't know. I just don't want your life to change. I don't want Bachan's life to get any harder. She's done so much for me already. She doesn't need this."

"Why are you trying to take all the blame? You want to blame someone? Blame me. It was my fault."

"It wasn't." Even now, I wanted him. In the shadows of my bedroom, I wanted him to hold me. I wanted to feel his skin on mine. My body ached with such longing, even though he was right there in front of me.

"It was my fault," he said again. "I shouldn't have rushed you. I would've waited for as long as you wanted me to." I couldn't help but smile to myself.

"Liar." I laughed. For a moment, the heaviness in the room lifted, and we could both breathe again.

"Look, I know we didn't plan this, but I want you to know that I'm happy. Maybe I won't amount to anything in my life. Maybe I'll always be less than the next guy, but at least I'd be a father, and I'd be with you. That's enough for me."

He smiled. He was truly happy. And now, I was going to ruin it all. I embraced him then. It wasn't because I felt the same way. I just didn't want him to see my face. I didn't want him to see how doubt had already taken over my heart.

"Tomorrow, we'll talk to Bachan properly. I'll make her understand."

I pulled away from him. "No, Naoki. I have to leave now. I've already caused enough trouble for your family."

"Where are you planning to go?"

"Back to my father's house where I belong."

"Are you crazy? After all that happened?"

"After all that happened."

"I'll go with you then. We'll find a place of our own." That was the thing about Naoki; his heart was deep, wide, and vast. He had room to love all of me, even the part that was running away from him, the part that was breaking his heart.

"No, let me go by myself. Bachan has already lost too much. She won't be able to go on without you. If I leave now, things can go back to normal around here. And I won't feel like such a burden."

"How can you say that?"

"Naoki. I don't deserve you."

"No, I'm not letting you go by yourself. I don't know what you'll do or when you'll come back. And I can't live with that."

"Don't you see, Naoki? Bachan will have to live with the fact that everyone will think I did this to you. People talk. Do you want that?"

"You don't know her, Nami. She would never believe them."

"You're her only grandson, her only family, the heir to this inn. You're all Bachan has left. You're important, Naoki. You're going to be someone."

He looked up and held my gaze. "So are you, Nami. You're going to be a mother."

I knew then that there was nothing I could say or do to change his mind. So, I gave in. I let him take off my clothes, run his hands over my skin. He covered me with his body. I ran my hands down his back. I couldn't wait. I wanted him inside of me. I wanted to be filled with that light. When he entered me, it took all of me not to cry out, to hold my screams inside. Whole eternities passed in that moment. Infinity times two. Afterwards, he held me for the rest of the night, and I believed him then when he told me that he would never let me go.

IT MUST HAVE BEEN CLOSE TO DAWN when I opened my eyes, but it seemed so much darker than it should've been. I reached for my daughter. She was still asleep, her chest rising and falling in a steady rhythm. But I couldn't hear her. In fact, I couldn't hear anything. It was that sensation of being underwater where every sound was muffled. Then, all at once, everything became clear. A car passed outside the inn. I could hear a train in the distance. And even in the middle of the city, the cicadas were chirping.

I was breathing heavily, as if I had traveled far to get here, wherever here was. When I looked up again, the stars were falling from the night sky. They landed on the soft powdered snow, glowing orange all around me. I blew out the air in a fog. I couldn't tell if I were awake anymore. My eyes were open, but it felt like I was still dreaming, still trying to find my way home.

"Nami-chan. Nami-chan." That voice came at me like a whisper and then sank down deep into my heart. "Nami-chan." I couldn't move. Tears filled my eyes. How long had it been since she last called my name?

My daughter stirred in her sleep, and the voice faded. If Naoki had been here, he would've gotten up. He would have held me in his arms, saying my name again and again until I stopped crying. *How I missed those arms around me!* That feeling of being safe, like nothing bad could ever happen again.

"Bad dreams?" he would say to me.

But this time, I would have told him that they weren't necessarily bad. It was more a feeling of sadness and heaviness that wouldn't leave me, even when I awoke. And the scent of pine trees that lingered in the air.

When I opened my eyes again, the sun was already up. I didn't have to see the clock to know that I was late. But I didn't want to get out of bed. For just a moment, I wanted to lie there. I wanted to believe that it wasn't just a dream, that it was really her, that after all this time, *she* was the one calling my name.

That day at the river, I wondered why it hadn't been her voice, why a complete stranger had saved me, why Naoki's voice had been so clear, it cut straight through to my heart.

"Nami-chan? Time to wake up. Breakfast is ready." I started to tear up. It should've been her calling me now, not Kana. It should've been her voice that day at the river. It should have been her who called me back from the water. But there was no time to dwell on those things now. The day had already started.

"I'm coming!"

By the time I got downstairs, everyone was seated, and the food was laid out in a myriad of pretty dishes. One glance, and I knew that she had made all my favorites.

"Bachan, I'm so sorry—"

"Come now, Nami. Sit down and eat."

"Mama," Suzu said. "Eat, eat!"

Bachan and I couldn't help but laugh. I missed that sound, the way it felt in my body. But even now, it seemed too soon to laugh, too soon to smile. I didn't know if I could ever be happy again.

"Were you able to get some sleep?" Bachan asked.

"I did." I could feel her eyes studying my face, and it took all of me not to cry. Naoki used to do the same thing. He knew, just by a look, if I were lying. So did she.

Her eyes came to rest on my wrist, but she didn't see the bruise that my father had left behind. "You're still wearing his watch," she said. Bachan reached out and gently touched the blue face. She looked at it fondly for a long time, as if it really were Naoki's face she was seeing. "But it doesn't work anymore."

"I know." In that moment, I couldn't bring myself to tell her that it didn't matter that the watch was broken. For me, time stopped the day Naoki died. Right now, I just needed something to hold onto, something to keep my head above water.

She smiled weakly. We didn't say anything for a while, each of us lost in our own thoughts, our own memories of him. I knew that she missed him terribly. So did I.

"You didn't have to go through all this trouble," I said to her, waving my hand over the breakfast spread.

"Nevermind."

"Bachan."

"Look, Nami. We can manage at the inn today, so take it easy. Rest. You don't have to help out."

"I want to, Bachan. It takes my mind off of things."

"I know."

"Plus, I don't know what to do about my father."

"You're not thinking of going back, are you? I told you, Naoki would never hold that against you. He wasn't like that."

"It's not that. I want to know what he knows. I want to know what really happened. And right now, he's the only one who can tell us."

"Nami."

"I need to know the truth, Bachan. Otherwise, I can't go on. I can't move forward." We both looked at Suzu, hoping she didn't understand.

"I don't want you to go back, Nami."

"I don't want to, either. But what choice do I have? He was the only other person in the valley at that time."

"But he was already too sick to leave the house. You remember what the detective said. It's impossible."

"Still, he has to know something."

Just then, Kana entered the room and made a beeline for Bachan.

"Okami, there's a man outside who would like to speak with Nami. He didn't want to give his name, but I'm almost certain that he's been here before."

Bachan patted my hand. "I'll take care of it, Nami. You just eat. Look, I made all of your favorites."

"No, Bachan. I'm fine, really."

"Kana, tell the gentleman to come inside. You can use my office, Nami."

"No, okami. The man would like to speak with her outside."

"It's okay, Bachan. I'll go."

"Are you sure?" Her eyes held mine for what felt like an eternity, but I looked away.

"Yes."

He was waiting in front of the inn. Even with his back turned to me, I could tell, he had aged. He was a little more bent over now, and his clothes hung on his body like a sigh. But I recognized him immediately.

"Mr. Aizawa?" He turned around and bowed.

"Oh, Nami-chan. It's been such a long time."

"It has."

When I looked up again, waiting for him to continue, he just stood there. I could tell from his furrowed brow and deep stare that he had so much he wanted to tell me, but it was like he couldn't find the right words to begin. Then, all of a sudden, I felt tears in my eyes.

He said it again. "You look so much like your mother." In that moment, I didn't think he realized what he had said. It was like he was talking in his sleep, the words falling from his lips before he could stop them. When he finally saw my face, he bowed low. "I'm very sorry."

Junichiro Aizawa had been my father's publisher when he first started out as a writer. But to me, Aizawa would always be much more than that. Whenever my father was too busy with his work, Aizawa always volunteered to take care of me. He would pick me up from school and make me dinner. He loved curry rice, so we ate that often. I was so young, but even now, I felt the warmth of those times.

By the time Aizawa was transferred to the main office in Tokyo, my father had already placed me in a new school in Kyoto City. During those years, I missed him desperately. It was like a part of me had already decided that he was my real father, and I was just waiting for him to return home to me. I sent him cards and letters, even though I knew that there was nothing he could do.

"I'm sorry to just show up like this, especially after all these years."

"No, it's good to see you."

"It's good to see you too, Nami. But it makes me wish that I were coming here under better circumstances."

"I don't understand."

"I don't know if you knew, but your father had been ill for the past year. It was a terrible illness, and he suffered a lot. But now, he's at peace. He died last night."

"No." I began to cry.

"I'm so sorry, Nami."

"Don't be." Those tears weren't for him. I was glad he was gone. I was glad he had suffered. But the thing is, now I would never know. I would never know why Naoki died. And the one person who could have told me was gone.

"I know that this has been a tough couple of months for you with your husband's passing and now your father. I don't want to make things more difficult, but I have to ask if you'd like to see him before he's cremated."

"No, that won't be necessary." I wiped the tears from my face.

"I know. I just wanted to ask as a courtesy. Just in case you may have changed your mind."

"Thank you, Mr. Aizawa. I'm sorry that my father left you to clean up his mess again."

"He was a troubled man, Nami. It was the least I could do. For the last month, he had been in the hospital. And there were so many days when he just wanted to go already. Breath is life, and when you can't get enough of it, you're not living, and he wasn't."

"Wait! You said that my father had been in the hospital for the last month?"

"That's correct."

"That can't be."

"Why do you say that?"

"I just saw him yesterday. I went to his house, and his nurse, Akane, let me in. I saw him lying there. He was in his room." I touched the bruise on my wrist.

"That's impossible, Nami. He's been in the hospital all this time, and as far as I know, he's never had a nurse named Akane."

In that moment, my head was spinning. I didn't know what to think. No matter what Aizawa was telling me now, I knew that I had met Akane. I had been inside that house. I had seen my father with my own eyes. I was sure of it.

"How could that be?" I said to myself.

"Look, Nami. I don't know what happened yesterday, but if you need to see the house again, to verify what you saw, I can give you the key." He reached into his pocket and pulled out a set of keys. One was small and silver, and the other was a large brass one for the gate. He put them in my hands and smiled.

"Thank you."

"I hope you find what you're looking for."

"Me too."

"If you need anything, I'll be at the house later today. I'll bring your father's ashes."

He put on his hat and turned to go. I walked him out into the street again.

"You know, Nami, your father was really trying hard to change. You might not have seen it yesterday, because he just wanted to go already. But about a year ago, he came to me with an idea for a new book. He wanted to do something for you, even if you wouldn't accept it. In his own way, he was trying to make things right again."

"That's hard to believe, even now."

"I know. But one day, you might change your mind. I don't know if he finished the book or if he was even going to publish it, but I just wanted you to know that the intent was there. He was trying to the very end to make amends."

"Thank you for telling me, Mr. Aizawa."

He bowed low. "Goodbye, Nami."

I watched him walk away until he disappeared around the corner. It was only then that in the quiet of the street, I felt my heart racing.

- 7 -

I STOOD IN FRONT OF THE INN long after Aizawa had left. Somewhere deep inside of me, I just couldn't bring myself to believe anything he had said. There was no way that the man I saw yesterday, the one who had grabbed onto my wrist, was just a figment of my imagination.

I rubbed the bruise underneath Naoki's watch. It was an ugly purple, and I could almost make out his fingerprints on my skin. *Was Aizawa telling me that this bruise was made by a ghost? And what about Akane? If she wasn't my father's nurse, then who was she? Who had called the inn?* Questions bloomed in my head like weeds. Soon, it was all overgrown, and I couldn't make sense of anything.

But just when I thought my heart would burst, I felt a tiny hand slip into mine. As small as it was, it was just enough to bring me back, to keep me from drifting out of this world.

"Mama?" I continued to smile at her even though those big dark eyes made me feel so sad.

"Hmm?"

"Who was that man you were talking to?"

"He was an old friend, Suzu, a dear old friend. He used to take care of Mama when I was your age." My heart warmed again with those precious memories. *How I wish life could have stayed in that happiness!*

"Did he make you curry rice?" I laughed in spite of myself.

"Yes, he did."

The two of us stood there for a moment, looking out into the street. In my mind, I saw Aizawa when he'd wait for me by the school gate. He always wore that flannel plaid hat, even as a younger man.

"Jichan!" I'd call out to him. Then I would run and leap into his arms. He always had a five o'clock shadow, so his cheek was rough against mine. He would always say that this is how a superhero's hair grows. But as strong as the hair was on his face, the hair on his head was that of a mere mortal. Even as a child, the irony of that was not lost on me.

"Did that man come here before?"

"He did. A long time ago, Suzu. Before you were even born."

The last time I saw Aizawa was not long after I had come to live in Kyoto City. Those first few months with Naoki and Bachan, I felt like I was slowly learning how to live again, how to breathe.

But that didn't last long. One day, out of the blue, my father showed up at the inn. He didn't come all the way from Kasumi-machi to apologize or make amends. He was there to take me home.

Just the sight of him outside made my skin crawl. He was pacing the street, back and forth, until he spotted me at the back entrance. He smiled. In an instant, I came face to face with those eyes, those eyes that hated me so much.

"Fox daughter," he whispered. I could feel his breath, hot against my skin. I turned away from him and shut my eyes. But he grabbed onto my wrist and began pulling me outside. I tried to scream, but who would hear me? Naoki had gone out to help Bachan. They weren't coming home any time soon. No matter how much he wanted to, Naoki couldn't save me now. I didn't know what to do. It was obvious that my father wasn't going home without me.

All at once, he put his face next to mine. He reeked of day-old alcohol. The sourness of his breath made me wince.

"That's right, Nami," my father cried. "You can't kill something that's part of your DNA. Once he finds out you're a fox, that boyfriend of yours won't want anything to do with you. Don't you see? Nothing good can come from a fox daughter." The way he spoke to me then, there was still such disdain in his voice. I could feel it.

He slowly pulled me out into the street. The farther I got from the inn, the more desperate I felt. My father wasn't going to let me go, no matter what anyone said. At that point, it seemed easier to just let him take me home. *Why fight back? Who would believe me?* I was just a child. He was my father, the famous writer. Everyone loved him.

But it was around that time when Aizawa showed up. My father had called him. He had wanted a ride.

"Isao! What are you doing?"

My father grinned at him. "I'm here to claim my prize." Aizawa met my eyes. In that moment, the horror in them was inexplicable.

"Let her go, Isao! You don't want to do this! She's your daughter!"

"Don't tell me what to do!" He sneered at Aizawa. "This one's going to be just like her mother. Fox daughter," he whispered into my ear.

This time, the words stung. I could feel my fists clench even though I was trembling with fear. *Had he forgotten how kind she was? How good a mother she had been? Didn't he know how much she loved him?* I knew she did. I was sure of it. My mother would never run away with another man. But even now, it was no use trying to convince him. He had already made up his mind.

"Isao! Enough of this!" Aizawa shouted. My father looked at him with the same hatred in his eyes.

"What do you know? You're not her father."

"I know. You are, Isao. So, start acting like it!" In that moment, he glared at Aizawa in a way that made me fear for his life. But Aizawa wasn't scared. He opened the car door and waited. My father stood there for a long time, not wanting to let go of me, not wanting to let Aizawa win. But eventually, he relented.

"I'm so sorry, Nami-chan," Aizawa said. I didn't know what to tell him in that moment, and he didn't wait for my reply. He just got in the car and slowly pulled away. I watched them leave. But my father's eyes never left me— even in my dreams.

"What did he want, Mama?"

"What did who want, Suzu?"

"That man."

"Nothing, Suzu. It was nothing." But as we turned to go inside, the weight of those keys sat heavy in my hand. They were pulling me back as much as my daughter was trying to move me forward. Deep down, I wondered who would win.

- 8 -

ALL MORNING, I COULD FEEL THE WEIGHT of those keys in my pocket. As I reached up to wipe the windows or bent down to vacuum under the tables, I could feel them dragging me back into the darkness. It didn't matter that my daughter had been so good all morning or that she had helped me clean the rooms and gotten them ready for new guests. Something was doing battle in my heart, and I was afraid that my father was winning.

By early afternoon, I had made up my mind.

"You want to go back?" Bachan asked. She took off her glasses and turned to look at me. "Why?"

"I just need to see the place with my own eyes."

"Is it because of Mr. Aizawa?"

I nodded. "I need to know if what I saw was real. I just can't shake the feeling that my father was somehow connected to Naoki's death."

"Nami. Do you really believe that?"

"Yes. I know firsthand what a man that cruel is capable of. If there was anyone who would hurt Naoki, it would be my father."

"But he's gone, Nami. Even Mr. Aizawa said that."

"I know it's useless, but I need to try for Naoki's sake, for my sake, for your sake and for Suzu. So please, Bachan, can you take care of Suzu just one more time. I'm so sorry to cause you so much trouble."

She stood up and grabbed my hands. "Nami-chan. It's no trouble, but promise me that you'll be safe. I want you to come home to me."

"I will."

But when it was time to leave, Suzu wouldn't have it. She wouldn't believe me. Her eyes watched me in the same way Naoki did. I couldn't escape them.

"Don't worry, Suzu-chan," I sang happily. "Before you know it, I'll be home again, and we'll go feed the fish together at Mr. Yamaguchi's pond."

"No!" she shouted. Her face was bright red, and tears were streaming down her cheeks.

"Suzu-chan. Listen to Mama. It'll only be for a little while. I promise."

"No! No! No! Mama won't be back." I pulled her into my arms, but she pounded my chest with her fists. No matter what I said, I couldn't convince her.

"Let her tire out," Bachan said. "It'll be okay, Nami."

Would it? Ever since Naoki died, Suzu watched me like her life depended on it. I tried to convince her that Naoki was still here. He was a star in the sky now. "All of us will one day turn into stars," I told her. "But Papa was so special that he went on ahead of us."

"And a very long time from now, I'll see him again?" she asked.

"Yes." At the time, that story seemed to work. But somewhere deep inside, I knew that Suzu could sense the unsteadiness of my heart. I was this planet that could fall off its axis at any moment, and she knew it. But I didn't want her to worry about me. I wanted her to believe in the beautiful story I told her about her father. I didn't want her to have to live with the truth, whatever it turned out to be. But there was no talking to her now.

"Bachan, I have to take her." I wiped Suzu's eyes with a handkerchief, and she buried her face in my chest.

"Nami-chan. She's just tired. Don't worry."

"No, I know Suzu, and she won't let this go." Bachan sighed. She was almost on the verge of tears. She held me by the shoulders and looked deep into my eyes.

"Be safe, okay? Come back to me, okay?"

"Don't worry, Bachan."

She saw us off in the front of the inn. What she must have seen was a young woman trying so hard to be brave and a little girl, who was desperately holding on. But like Naoki, I didn't turn back.

At Kyoto Station, we waited for the bus to Kasumi-machi. Suzu was already asleep, her head resting on my lap. I was grateful not to see her eyes staring back at me, piercing my heart, indicting me. She reminded me so much of Naoki. I can still feel the way he looked at me that day. For as long as I live, I'll never forgive myself for the pain I caused him.

That day at the river, I had promised him. He made me lock pinkies and swear that I'd live no matter what. But each day that passed, I was finding it harder and harder to keep my promise to him. He didn't know what was going on, and at the time, I couldn't tell him. I thought the best thing to do was to push him away.

"You don't have to wait with me at the station," I told him. I tried to sound like I didn't care, but I underestimated

Naoki's heart. When I glanced up at him and met his gaze, I could see that pained expression in his eyes.

"But I always wait with you."

"I know. But Sugiwara offered. He lives closer to me. It'll just be easier, you know?"

"Fine," he said. "If that's what you want, I'll leave." He stormed away. In my heart, a part of me felt relieved. Something was changing. It was like that cheeriness, that light that had begun to grow inside my heart, was starting to fade away. I didn't want Naoki to see it happen.

But I was certain that he knew. After that day at the river, his eyes never left me. He was always waiting for me to say something, to share with him anything. But I just couldn't. I didn't want him to know. I didn't want to get him involved. And even that day at the river, he didn't ask.

No matter what I had said, when afternoon came and school was over, Naoki showed up at Kyoto Station.

"What are you doing here?" I was so surprised to see him that I could hardly get the words out. "I told you, you don't have to worry. Sugiwara is going to take me home." My heart was in a panic now.

"No, I'll take you home," he said as he tried to take my hand. But I wouldn't let him. I stood there, tears already in my eyes.

"No, you don't have to," I cried. I was pleading with him now. But he wouldn't listen.

"I just want to make sure you get to Kasumi-machi all right." That's what he said at first, that he'd only ride the bus with me. He would only walk as far as the rice fields. Then it was to the rise in the road. But that day, he ended up walking me home, all the way, deep into the heart of the valley. And he didn't stop until we reached my father's house.

- 9 -

THAT RAINY NIGHT WHEN I HAD COME TO LIVE with Naoki and
Bachan, I vowed that I'd never return to Kasumi-machi
again. But no matter how hard I tried, I couldn't escape the
scent of cedar trees in the air, the darkness of the pine forest
across the bridge, and the sound of water everywhere, even
in my dreams. I realized that while I had tried hard to forget
my hometown, it had never once forgotten about me.

When we finally got off the bus, the warm wind of the
valley rushed to greet us. It embraced me so tightly I could
hardly breathe.

"Mama," I whispered. For a moment there, I missed the
Kasumi-machi in my heart. It was the home of my mother,
of everything good that had happened while she was here.
The expanse of blue sky above, the green valley walls that

climbed all the way up to the heavens, and even the cicadas welcomed me home. I was a child under that summer sun, and in that light, even I, could hope again.

I took Suzu's hand, and she smiled at me. Everything that had happened back at the inn seemed to have been forgotten. Her gaze had softened, and in those eyes, I saw Naoki again, the way I wanted to remember him. He was with me now, as he had always been, and together, we set out along the rice fields. As far as our eyes could see, the valley floor was covered in green. In a few months, it would all turn golden. It would be the time of the harvest. And every light that had burned to its brightest in summer would begin to fade. But I didn't want to think about that yet.

The clouds were moving across the sky. I could see their paths reflected in the rice paddies below. At the edge of the forest, the afternoon light began to descend inside, and the scent of cedar trees lilted on the breeze all around us. I closed my eyes. Even now, I could hear it. The river was calling to me.

"What is it, Mama?" I looked into my daughter's dark eyes and smiled.

"It's nothing."

Eventually, the town of Kasumi-machi was behind us, and we were in the heart of the valley. There were few homes here. The quiet descended around us like a blanket. When we reached the rise in the road, I knew it wouldn't be long now. The sound of water was everywhere.

From where I stood, I could already see the roofline of my father's house. It didn't matter how much time had passed. I would never forget the way back. And that day, neither had Naoki.

We stood outside the gate, neither one of us saying goodbye. I wanted to tell him that I wished time would stop, that I wanted to be with him in this moment forever. But I couldn't say it. I couldn't bring myself to tell him what was waiting for me inside. All I could do was stand there, my eyes pooling with tears.

As I turned to leave, he pulled me into his arms. He wasn't trying to comfort me exactly. He wanted me to know that he liked me, loved me even. But I didn't hug him back. It was like I didn't know how. He didn't deserve someone like me. Still, his heart beat hard against my chest. In that moment, I knew that he didn't want to let me go.

All of a sudden, my father appeared outside. I didn't know how long he had been standing there, or how much he had seen, but once I saw him, I quickly pulled away. Naoki bowed, but my father didn't acknowledge him. He just stood there with those cold eyes, bloodshot and glassy.

I put my hands in my pockets. I didn't want Naoki to see that I was trembling. I smiled at him.

"I'll see you tomorrow, okay?" I told him, trying to make him believe that nothing was wrong.

"Promise?"

"Yes, I promise." I watched as he turned and began heading back down the valley road. He kept looking back, and I kept waving to him for as long as I could. Eventually, he had gotten so small in my vision, far away like a mirage, that I told myself he wasn't real. After that, the last thing I heard was the gate slam behind me.

"Mama!" Suzu cried. She tugged at my arm. I looked at her as if I were coming back from a dream.

An eternity had passed, but I hadn't moved. My eyes were still fixed on the front gate. It was heavy and made of dark wood. Just the sight of it made me angry. If I had my way, I'd tear it down with my bare hands. I'd set the whole place on fire if that would erase him from my memory. But not before I knew the truth.

"Yes, Suzu."

"Aren't we going inside?"

"Of course." I took the brass key from my pocket and unlocked the gate. In that moment, I couldn't help but notice her absence. I expected to see Akane, cutting hydrangea blossoms and greeting me with a warm smile.

There was no one to welcome me today. In fact, the garden looked as though no one had lived here in months. The hydrangea was gone. All that was left were a few bonsai plants growing wild and unruly along the perimeter. It was only my father's house that remain unchanged—my own silent witness. Maybe to a stranger, his house was beautiful. Shoji doors and a wraparound veranda made it look like a humble Japanese shrine. But there was nothing holy about it. Even now, it was just an accomplice.

That day, when the gate slammed behind me, there was no time to think. My father had already grabbed my arm and was dragging me toward the house. I didn't want to go inside. I didn't think I could endure it any longer. There was something about the way Naoki had embraced me that day. It was like I could still feel his love there on my body, imprinted like an amulet. I tried to hold onto that feeling, but it was no use. My father overpowered me. He pulled me into the house and shut the door.

In that moment, I was screaming inside, but nothing came out of my mouth. My father grabbed me by the arms and shook me hard. He was pressing so hard into my flesh I thought I was going to pass out.

"Who do you think you are, parading around with a boy like that?" He threw me down onto the floor. He was so angry inside. It was like he couldn't control it already. He was wringing his hands and pacing the floor. I tried to inch away from him. When I couldn't move any further, I huddled into a ball, praying he'd stop. But he didn't.

In an instant, he was in my face again, the stench of alcohol making me dizzy. "Did you ever think about me? Fox daughter. Answer me!" That's when I heard it. Even now, it amazed me how much a slap at full force resembled a kind of explosion.

"I'm sorry, Papa. It won't happen again."

"Of course, it won't happen again. I won't let it. Not this time. Why did you leave? Why did you leave?!" He bent down and touched my face gently. But by that time, I didn't trust that tenderness. I was crying so hard that I couldn't see his face. "Sanae."

He began to stroke my hair, just like the last time. I froze. I wanted to tell him, "I'm Nami! Don't you see? I'm your daughter!" But he was too far gone to believe me. When he reached for me and began to unbutton my shirt, I just let him. It was easier this way. The wounds stayed on the inside. No one would ever see it. And if they didn't see it, I wouldn't have to explain. To speak it out loud made it real, and I didn't want it to be.

But from the corner of my eye, I saw Naoki by the door. I turned away quickly. I couldn't look at him. I didn't want him to see me like this. I didn't want him to know what was going on, to see how dirty I was! By that time, my father had noticed him too. He let go of me. I moved away from him, clenching at my shirt.

Naoki didn't hesitate. He ran at my father with all his might and tackled him to the floor. If I hadn't been there, he probably would have killed him. I could see it in his eyes, that hatred. Instead, he punched him in the stomach with all the strength of a fourteen-year-old boy. My father writhed in pain, but he never stopped glaring at me.

Naoki grabbed my hand, but I couldn't move. *Didn't he see?* This was where I belonged. It was my fault that she was gone. I felt so ashamed.

"Just go, Naoki," I said to him. There were tears in his eyes.

"Nami. Why didn't you tell me?" I couldn't answer him. *What would I have said?* Naoki wasn't going to wait for me to explain. He pulled me up. "It's okay, Nami. You're safe now."

In no time, we had escaped through the front gate and made it back to the valley road. And we didn't stop running until we could no longer see my father's house.

By the time we reached Kyoto, it was raining.

‐ 10 ‐

I SLID THE DOOR OPEN. Standing in that entryway again, the scent of cedar wood crashed down on me like a wave. I squeezed Suzu's hand. All I wanted to do in that moment was run, but when my daughter looked at me, I couldn't turn away. In her eyes, I saw Naoki, urging me on. I knew that I had to keep going, that I wouldn't be able to live with myself without knowing what happened to him.

Still, I didn't want to be here. The house felt like it had been shuttered for months. The air was stale and each step we took echoed through that emptiness as if we were in a cave. In that moment, I missed Akane. She had made it easier to be here. She had brought light to the darkness. Without her, I was beginning to feel desperate. My heart was already pounding in my ears. Too much longer, and I'd surely drown.

I let go of Suzu's hand and ran ahead. I pushed open the shoji doors and then the shutters. Moments later, the harsh afternoon light flooded the room. The shadows disappeared, and the dust plumed and glinted in the sun's rays. Suddenly, I could feel it, that warm wind of the valley returning, circling around us like an embrace.

All at once, I was in the field again, the yellow flowers bobbing in the wind like little suns. The sun was shining that day, the sky, a crisp blue. Little by little, the yellow bouquet in my tiny hands grew too big for me.

"Nami-chan!" I turned at the sound of her voice.

"Mama?" She was singing that song she always sang, the one I loved. My mother was laughing now. But no matter where I looked, I couldn't find her. The sound of water filled my ears.

"Nami-chan!" And then everything fell silent.

"Mama." I felt her name fall from my lips, but I wasn't in the field anymore. I was in the house again. I was standing on the engawa. I couldn't understand it. She sounded like she was right here with me. *What was happening?* I shook my head. I didn't know what to think. Then I saw the garden.

What lay before me now was not what I saw yesterday. The pine tree that had once soared to the sky was bent over like an old man, shouldering what was left of the maples. There was no greenery left. The ground was littered with dead pine needles and dried leaves. The hydrangeas were gone. Not even that twilight blue remained. The weeping willow had cried until it was dry, and the large fishpond was now empty. Seeing the garden like this, I wanted to cry. *Had yesterday been just a dream?*

I turned back to the room. The black lacquered table where Akane had served me tea and sweets, was crowded with empty green tea bottles, an ashtray of half-smoked cigarettes, and a mess of papers with my father's writing scribbled across it. I saw my name written on one of the pages, but it had been crossed out, and there were no other words. Even in death, he could think of nothing good to say about me.

"Mama," Suzu called. She was standing by the family altar, holding a small picture in her hands. "Is this you?" I looked at the black and white image, taking it from her and gently cradling it in my palm. It was a picture of my mother, sitting in the garden. She was smiling as if she were just starting her life, as if a myriad of possibilities were spread out before her. *That could have been me.* To have gotten to that age with a smile on her face, I couldn't help but feel envious.

"No, it's not me, Suzu." I looked at the picture again.

She must have loved the person who had captured her image. I could see it in her eyes. But I couldn't believe that it was the same man.

My father told me that he was going to burn all of her things. I had watched as he gathered everything together and lit it on fire in the garden. Even now, I remember how big the flames were, licking the air, threatening to burn his face. But he only stood there, watching until the embers were all that were left of my mother. He told me that he was doing it for my sake, that the best thing I could do was to forget about her. At the time, I couldn't blame him.

The rumors began not long after my mother had left. My father couldn't take me anywhere in the town without seeing the looks of pity and hearing them whisper behind his back. "Poor thing," they said. "He was fooled by a fox." At the time, I didn't know if he was listening. My father was too busy just trying to survive.

When I close my eyes, I can still hear him at the bridge. He went back there every morning. He called out my mother's name again and again, but no matter how many times he called to her, she wouldn't be found. He searched everywhere. He bowed and pleaded in front of many people to please take a look at her picture once more. But no one remembered her.

As the months passed, his resolve was slipping. I could hear it in his voice, the way he called her name. That was the thing about rumors, wasn't it? Eventually, all stories became one, and that one story, told all the time was a hundred times more powerful than the truth.

After a while, even my father believed them.

It was easy to think that my mother was a fox. She was extraordinarily beautiful, much more so than any other woman in the town. That was a fox's best trick, to make a man believe it was a woman. Men were weak for beauty, so it was easy. But it was only a matter of time before a fox would play tricks on him or even humiliate him. At worst, she'd take his soul.

To my father, my mother would always be a fox. And if he were right, then that made me a fox daughter. It was in my blood to ruin everything. I knew that Naoki and Bachan would have denied it. They would probably tell me again and again how I wasn't like her, how my father had been mistaken. But even now, I knew better.

After my mother left, I began to grow more and more in my father's image. Everyone in the town said it, and when they did, I felt like they were relieved. My father felt the same way. Yes, Mama had vanished. People could say what they wanted. They could make up their own stories. But when they saw me in person, there was no doubt that I was his child.

But didn't he know? My mother's face was sleeping just below the surface.

I didn't notice it at first. *How could I?* I had been too young to hold onto that memory of her. With each passing year, my mother's face was fading little by little. I couldn't even remember the fine details anymore. But my father had never forgotten.

I had watched him burn all of my mother's things. I had seen the ashes swept up by the wind and taken far far away. My father had told me himself that she was gone, that there was nothing left to remember her by. But I knew that wasn't true.

I peered into the small mirror hanging on the wall. Then I turned back to the picture in my hands. It was a little faded, but I could still see it. The moment I found her picture hidden under my father's pillow, I realized what he had seen all along. It was the same square jawline, the same heart lips, and those eyes that seemed to dance if she smiled. No matter how much I didn't want it to be true, the mirror didn't lie. My features were my mother's, exactly.

I didn't know when he had realized it, but sometime after I had turned twelve, my father began to look at me differently. When I was in the garden, feeding the fish, or especially, when I was sitting on the stone bench where my mother had often spent her time, his eyes would linger. Sometimes, he would even call me by my mother's name. But I wouldn't answer him.

Eight years have already passed. I became a wife and a mother, but I can't escape those feelings, no matter how hard I try. Even now, my face still burns with shame when I think about that day.

My father opened the door to the bath by accident.

"I'm sorry," he said to me, but he didn't look away. I didn't want him to see my pain, so I sunk down deeper into the water, submerging my whole face. The tears came then. They mixed with the bath water.

I remember thinking then that the sea must be such a lonely place, just sitting there, collecting everyone's tears. I felt sorry for it, that all I could give it was my grief.

When I came to the surface again, he was gone. In that moment, I could have told myself that it was just a dream, just some made-up story in my head. But I knew that wasn't true. No matter what I did, I couldn't erase the fact that he had been there.

- 11 -

IN THE MIDDLE OF THE NIGHT, when it was so quiet that I could hear the river, the moonlight stole inside. It inched its way across the tatami, getting closer and closer to where I was sleeping. I tried to reach for that light. But the shoji doors slid closed, and the room went dark again. My heart was beating so loud, I couldn't hear the river anymore. I was afraid he would hear it in that silence, that it would give me away. But it didn't matter. Moments later, I felt his hand brush against my cheek.

"Sanae," he whispered. His face was so close to mine now that the stench of his breath made me dizzy. He began to stroke my hair, just like the last time. I froze. I told myself that he just missed my mother, that he didn't mean to hurt me. But I couldn't convince my heart. When his hand slipped under my shirt, I wanted to scream, but by that time, I had already learned to be quiet. It was the only way to save myself.

"I missed you so much," he told me. "Why did you leave me, Sanae? Why?" He began to stroke my breasts. My nipples became hard. Even in the darkness, I could feel it in the air. He was smiling. Hot tears flowed from my eyes in a steady stream. In that moment, I wished that he could have seen my face. Maybe if he had, he would've stopped. Maybe he would have realized his mistake, that I wasn't my mother after all. But this time, his hand slid down over my stomach.

Fox daughter.

Maybe this is what I deserved. It was my fault, wasn't it? I was the one who wanted to see the bridge. I was the one who had begged my mother over and over again until she grew weary, until she could no longer say no. *Didn't he tell me never to go there? Wasn't it because of me that my mother was gone, and his life was ruined?*

By the time I opened my eyes, the dawn was waiting for me outside. I glanced over at my father. In the morning light, he didn't look like a monster anymore. I could pretend that he was my dear father. And he was. But even after he apologized and promised never to do it again, I knew he would break that promise every single time. I would never be able to trust him again.

I got up and rushed outside. I opened the gate and ran as hard as I could, down the slope, along the riverbank until I came to the edge of the bridge. My eyes searched far across to the other side, deep into the old pine forest.

"Mama," I whispered to myself. *How I missed her!* If she had stayed here, none of this would have ever happened. "Mama!" I cried at the top of my lungs, but my voice got lost in the rushing current.

In that moment, I could hear nothing else. The sound of water was in my ears, and it pulled me down to the river until I was standing in its shallows. I was frantic by then. I scrubbed my body until my skin was raw. But no matter how much I tried, I knew that I'd never be clean again.

I stared at the surface of the water. It shimmered blue. I wanted so badly to let go. What I wouldn't do to hear that silence at the bottom of the river again. But I couldn't bring myself to do it. I remembered my promise to Naoki. I would live, no matter what. *He should have left me at the bottom of that river. I should have drowned that day.*

My mother's scent floated on the breeze. It was the perfume of those yellow flowers that grew by the bridge. All at once, I wanted to be there in that field again. I wanted to see the fox shrine, the one that she had showed me that very day.

I bent down and smiled at Suzu. "Let's go pick some flowers for your grandmother." She smiled for the first time in what felt like months and reached for my hand.

"Let's go, Mama."

As we walked along the river together, I found myself singing that song again, the one my mother always sang when I was a child. Her voice was so clear now. It lilted and traveled on the breeze as I ran along beside her. She told me again about the field of flowers, how they looked like little suns, how they bobbed in the wind. She told me about the fox shrine and how she prayed to Inari. All I wanted was to see it with her, but I had promised my father never to go near the bridge.

But that morning, he had left for Kyoto City. It was a perfect opportunity. The two of us could go there together and no one would have to know. We would be back home safe in no time. My mother had refused me many many times. She had grown weary with my requests. But on that day, when the summer sky was so blue, she relented.

"Maybe for just a little while," she said.

I jumped up and down with joy and flew to the back gate. My mother got her red umbrella, but she didn't join me immediately. Instead, she was looking back at the house. She stared at it for a long time as if she were trying to imprint her whole life in her heart. I didn't notice it that day, but I realized over the years that the look on her face was one of nostalgia. In that moment, she knew something was going to happen. She knew that everything before her was going to become a memory.

That day at the bridge, I was the only one there with my mother, the only one who really knew what had happened. But when I tried to explain it to my father, I couldn't find the right words. After all, I was just a child.

"Nami, talk to me. Tell me, where did Mama go?" He held me by the arms. He was squeezing so hard that it hurt. Later, the welts came to the surface, blooming like flowers.

He asked me many times that day and the days that followed where my mother had gone. But no matter how many times I told him; he wouldn't believe me. I don't even think he trusted me anymore. I couldn't blame him. He must have felt like I was keeping my mother's secret. As time went on, I began to doubt my memory. I began to believe that it didn't happen.

Then one night, not long after my mother left, my father stood on the bridge, leaning over the railing. He wept then with such deep sadness that I didn't know what to do. I didn't know how to comfort him. It was the first time I had seen my father cry, and the sight of him there made me feel so uncomfortable, so helpless.

"Why?! Why?!" He must have gone on like that for just a few minutes, but it felt like an eternity to me. Eventually, he stumbled his way off the bridge and followed the river back to the house. I ran ahead of him. I slipped into the forest, careful not to let him see me or know that I was there.

By the time he returned, I was already waiting for him in the garden. I held my breath. When the gate unlatched and he staggered over to me and fell down, I instinctually moved to help him up. But I stopped myself. All of a sudden, he pushed himself up to his full height and brought his face right in front of mine. I had never seen a look of such hatred in my life.

"It was you," he said. His breath blew in my face like a sewer. "You were the reason Mama disappeared." I shook my head. Tears were rolling down my cheeks.

"No, Papa."

"I told you not to play on the bridge! I told you! But you didn't listen to me! Why didn't you listen to me?! You promised!" He screamed that last line in my face so loud, I thought I'd fall over. I couldn't stop shaking. Then my father teetered toward me for a second before he collapsed onto the garden floor. I didn't waste any time. I dashed out of the gate and ran down the slope. And I didn't stop running until I reached the river.

The rain had fallen steadily earlier in the afternoon, but now, the skies were clear, and the night was alive with stars. There was no moon, but I wasn't afraid. I had often walked along the river at night, the sound of the water soothing my heart. It was here that I could breathe again, that I could hope again. I stood at the riverbank and gazed up at the stars. They twinkled in my direction as if it were my mother saying hello.

"Mama," I whispered into the darkness. But she didn't answer. The stars were just the stars again and nothing more. In that moment, I felt the weight of my loneliness, how that feeling sat heavy in my heart.

"Nami-chan!" Hours later, my father's voice pierced the darkness. I could hear him call my name as if I had once again become someone dear to him. Eventually, I left the river and returned to the house, but I would never trust my father again. I knew then that he blamed me for what had happened to my mother. And as a child, I only knew how to carry that burden, not give it back to him.

- 12 -

I DREAMT OF MY MOTHER all throughout my pregnancy. I'd wake up, in the middle of the night, thinking that I heard her singing. It's impossible, I know. But her voice was so clear to me, like she was right there in the room. I wanted to see her so badly. I wanted to talk with her again like when I was little. *Didn't she know?* I was going to be a mother when I wasn't done being a child. I needed her to comfort me. I needed her to tell me that everything was going to be all right.

But all those doubts and insecurities seemed to fade away when Suzu was born. She was perfect. Ten fingers and ten toes with a laugh that tickled our hearts. When I held her in my arms, I remember thinking how beautiful she was. She looked like Naoki all over. In fact, there was barely a trace of me in her face. I was glad. My face would only be a burden. And I didn't want her to have to carry that, ever.

My daughter was this gift from the gods. She gave me purpose in my life. She was my reason for living. Back then, I thought that I'd always love her, that I would do anything to protect her. What I didn't realize is, how easy it is to make promises when things are good. After I lost Naoki, I couldn't save myself, not even for my daughter's sake. Instead, I let myself drown in my own loss. My love for Suzu only worked because Naoki had been right here with me. There was no other way.

Even now, I felt sorry for my daughter. She was trying so hard to carry my grief. I was her mother. I was supposed to be the one to dry her tears, to hold her close and tell her that everything was going to be all right. But all I did was drag her down. And I hated myself for it.

As we walked along the river, we came upon the field of flowers. Suzu ran ahead. Before I knew it, she was standing there in the middle of those yellow blossoms, shining so bright that I couldn't help but feel envious. I wanted to shine again. I wanted to feel that light hum inside of me. But being back in Kasumi-machi, the darkness felt too heavy to bear.

"Mama? Mama?" Suzu had stopped what she was doing, and her eyes locked onto mine.

"Yes?"

"Do you hear that?"

"Hear what, Suzu?" I lied. But my eyes were already searching in the direction of the bridge, the river, the forest. *Where was it coming from?*

"Mama?"

All at once, it grew louder. I wanted to tell Suzu that she wasn't just imagining things, that I, too, could hear her as clear as day. But there was no time. I had to find her. She had to be here, her voice like a beacon leading me home.

"Mama? Is that you?" I whispered. In an instant, I had grabbed Suzu's hand, and we flew up the slope and back into the cedar forest. I didn't notice the afternoon light streaming through the trees or the wind on my skin. I didn't even smell the cedar in the air. No, this time, I ran as if my life depended on it.

Soon, the river became a murmur, and my mother's song bloomed in that hushed forest. Her voice was so clear now. She had to be here. It would be too cruel if she weren't. But no matter how hard I looked, not a single soul remained in that forest, except me and Suzu.

I couldn't understand it. She sounded so close, like she was standing right there next to me. It couldn't have been a dream. *How long had it been since I let myself escape to the forest? When had I even allowed myself to hope?* Now, her voice was everywhere, but I couldn't find her. Emotion welled up in my chest.

"Mama, look!"

I quickly wiped away my tears. "What is it, Suzu?"

"Look!" she cried. My heart was pounding in my chest. I turned around expecting to see my mother. But it wasn't her. Peering out from behind a cedar tree was a pure white fox. Her eyes twinkled when they met mine. I sank down to the forest floor. Without any hesitation, she came to me, and licked my palm, as if to say, "Welcome home."

In the middle of the night, when I couldn't fall asleep, that fox would be waiting for me outside the back gate of my father's house. I wasn't afraid, even back then. When I would hold out my hand, she would come to me and lick my palm as if she already knew me. She stayed as long as I wanted. She let me pet her coarse fur. How could I not feed her? She was all that I had left of my mother.

Then one night, the white fox didn't show up. I waited for hours, but the dawn was approaching. I needed to go inside. But when I turned back toward the house, I froze. Then, I was running.

"Mama!" I cried. She was sitting on the veranda, gazing up at the moon. She put her finger to her lips. "Where did you go, Mama?" I whispered.

My mother shook her head and smiled. She hugged me tight. I could feel her arms around me. It wasn't just a dream. She was really here.

But by the time I got up that morning, Mama was gone. I didn't want to believe it. My mother felt so real in my arms. I wanted to tell my father. I wanted him to believe me. I wanted him to tell me that it wasn't just a dream. But by then, it was too late. I had already learned how to be quiet.

After that, the fox never came again.

"You have to be careful of the foxes." His voice came at me from long ago. He wasn't angry yet. Underneath those words, his heart was still wounded and tender. He still missed my mother terribly. "Whatever you do, never follow a fox into the forest. It may appear to be a kind soul, but it isn't. Trust me, it isn't."

Over time, my father's advice turned into a warning. I didn't want to believe him. Mama wasn't a fox. *Didn't he see?* But when everyone in the village believed that my mother was a fox woman, he became vigilant. He didn't want me to end up like her. But it was too late.

When I looked up again, the fox was gone. Even the feel of her fur felt like a phantom in my hands. I searched the area, my eyes looking between cedar trunks and shadows, but it was useless. She was gone. I stood there in the middle of the forest, not knowing what to do next or where to go. I felt as though something precious had been returned to me for just a second and then ripped away again. It was too cruel. But in that moment, I felt a tiny hand slip into mine. I looked down at my daughter and tried my best to smile.

"It's okay, Suzu. It was nothing." But when I looked up again, I realized that there was something familiar about where we were. And then, up ahead, I could see it. There was a group of trees tightly clustered together. I couldn't believe it. After all this time, my heart still knew the way. "I didn't forget, Mama," I whispered.

I stood at the entrance to that grove, and ran my hand down the smooth bark of one of the trees. It was cold to the touch, but I needed that. With each step, the circle of cedars wound into a tight labyrinth, and the closer I got to the center, the more I felt like I was losing my tether to this world. But I didn't care. The incense was already burning in the air.

The scent of sandalwood began to fade. I had to hurry. I knew it wouldn't be long now. Just a few steps more and I'd be there. But when I finally reached the heart of the labyrinth, I almost cried out. I didn't know what was real anymore.

Where the old pine should have been, a mere shell of it remained. The trunk was almost completely hollowed out, and when I peered inside, I realized that what I had been looking for was missing. In that moment, I fell to my knees and began turning up the underbrush and dead leaves. But no matter how much I searched, I couldn't find it.

I crumpled to the ground, tears streaming down my cheeks. My heart didn't want to believe it. It had to be here. It was all I had left of my mother. Deep down, I had always held out hope that she would come back for me, that one day, the two of us would be together again. When I closed my eyes, I could still see her from the bridge. I could still hear her calling my name.

"Nami!"

I stared at the empty trunk where the fox shrine should have been. I remembered that day, how Mama took me to the shrine for the very first time.

"The foxes waited for me here," she said to me. Her gaze grew very far away. Up until then, I hadn't realized just how much my mother missed that shrine.

"Did Papa pray here too?"

"Nami, you cannot ever tell Papa about this place. It's our secret, okay?" I nodded. My mother was rarely firm with me, so it was so strange how serious she became. She took the bouquet from my hands and placed it in the vase next to the fox statue. Deep down, I wanted to promise her. I wanted my mother to trust me. But I was a child. I couldn't understand why we couldn't tell my father. He would have understood. I was sure of it.

"I promise, Mama," I said to her finally. My mother burned incense, and then put her hands together and prayed.

"What should we wish for, Mama?" I turned and Suzu was sitting down beside me, holding her bouquet in her hands. She was waiting for me to answer, but I didn't know what to say. There was no shrine. It was gone. *How had she known?* "Mama?" I looked into her eyes. There were so many things that I wanted to wish for, so many things that I wanted to be true.

Finally, I put my hands together and Suzu did the same. "Long life," I said to her. "Let's wish for long life." That was what my mother always wished for.

To this day, I still don't know why I did it. My mother told me before we left the house, "Nami-chan, stay by

Mama, okay? You have to listen to me now." I promised her. I gave her my word. But in the end. I couldn't keep it.

Maybe it was because I was here with Mama. Maybe it was because we were here together in this place for the very first time. But in that moment, the sound of water grew so loud I couldn't hear anything else. I shot out of the forest, through the field of flowers. And in no time, I was on the bridge.

"Nami!" my mother cried. But she was no match for the river. I was lost in its voice, the current rushing below me. I couldn't believe that I was suspended above such a force. It was exhilarating. I waved to my mother. I stepped up onto the railing to get a better view. "Nami!"

I could see my mother's face now, red with tears. *Why was she crying?* In that moment, I didn't stop to think about her. I didn't think about what I had promised her. All I knew was, the river had engulfed me. No one else could compete, not even my mother. She must have known this too. But she kept running. I could see her. She was so close now. We would be together soon. Finally, my mother was at the bridge.

And then, all of a sudden, I was alone.

When I opened my eyes, Suzu and I were standing at the edge of the bridge. I looked far across to the pine forest on the other side. It looked ominous, even in the day time.

All I heard was my mother desperately calling my name and the silence that fell upon the valley after she disappeared. I could still hear her geta walking away from me.

The river rushed below me. I couldn't escape it. Even now, the sound of water made my heart hurt. And there was nothing I could do to soothe it.

- 13 -

WE STARTED BACK ALONG THE RIVER. By that time, the sun was dropping in the afternoon sky, and soon the night would begin to settle in. I knew we had to hurry. Aizawa would be at the house soon, and I didn't want to miss him. But the last of the light fell softly on my back like a warm hand. My heart was hurting. On the breeze, I could smell the scent of those yellow flowers calling me back, begging me, *don't go.*

If I had my way, I'd stay here forever. I would search for Mama until it was too late, until I had no choice but to join Naoki on the other side. But when I looked at Suzu, I was reminded of what I had already done. I had only thought of myself. I had only cared about my own pain. Now, I would never escape that guilt.

I tugged at her hand again, but she wouldn't move. Something had caught her eye in the distance.

"Mama, look!" she cried. I turned back to where she was pointing, but the sun was too bright, its reflection dazzling on the surface of the water. I climbed up the slope, my eyes peering into that brightness.

All at once, he appeared, a lone shadow on the bridge, his white fur illuminated by the dying light. I couldn't believe it. *How long had it been since I last saw him?* From where I stood, he still felt like a dream. I had to get closer. I had to see his eyes. I needed to know if he were real.

As if she had read my mind, my daughter broke free and began running toward the bridge. "Suzu! Suzu!" I cried, but she was deaf to my voice. I felt myself running, the river and the forest becoming a blur. But no matter how much I pushed myself, my body felt like it was trying to run through water. All I could do now was watch as she kept getting farther and farther away from me.

Before I knew it, she was almost at the bridge. "Suzu, wait!" My legs were burning. My lungs were on fire. By that time, I couldn't even catch my breath. I was screaming inside. I was begging the gods to help me.

When she stopped at the edge, my heart whispered a silent thank you. But I wasn't relieved. Not yet. I knew that look. I could see it in her eyes. They were fixed on something just on the other side of the bridge. I wanted to see what she was looking at, what was making her act that way. I wanted to know if what I saw earlier was real. I took my eyes off of her for just a second. In that moment, I saw that flash of white fur disappear into the forest. I wasn't dreaming. It was him.

By the time I turned back, my daughter was already racing across the bridge. And no matter how many times I called to her, she wouldn't stop. I couldn't understand it. Why couldn't she hear me? "Suzu!"

The river roared below me, but I wouldn't listen to its warnings. I had to get to my daughter. I wasn't going to lose her to the forest. But the weight of my grief was too heavy. I couldn't carry it on my own. In the end, all I could do was watch as the forest swallowed her whole.

"Suzu!"

No matter how much fear had taken over my heart, I knew I had to keep going. I had to find her. In that moment, I didn't think about my mother or that day when she vanished from the bridge. I didn't think about how dark that pine forest was or how they said that you could lose your mind if you went inside alone. All I thought about was my daughter.

Once I stepped inside, the darkness enveloped me. It felt thick and old like it had always been this way. When my eyes finally adjusted to the absence of light, I moved deeper into the forest, where the scent of damp earth and pine trees seemed to grow stronger with each step. By that time, my head was spinning. I steadied myself against one of the trees and pressed my cheek against its trunk. The bark was cool against my skin. And in that darkness, I felt a small bit of comfort.

But I knew I couldn't stop. My eyes scanned the forest. I was sure that the sun had set by now. There was a bite in the air. I could feel it. And it was only going to get worse. If the cold had already gotten under my skin, my daughter must have been freezing. I couldn't imagine her lasting the night in this place. And frankly, I didn't have much hope for myself.

"Suzu! It's Mama! Where are you?" I called out again, but my voice felt too loud, as if I were yelling at a shrine. I didn't care. I needed to find her. I couldn't give up now.

But no matter how hard I tried, the silence continued to mock me. I listened as hard as I could for any small cry, any footsteps, but there were few sounds here. No birds or bird songs, only the scurrying of hidden animals in the underbrush or my own footsteps on the forest floor. The river was close by, but I couldn't hear it anymore.

It was so dark here under the dense canopy of pines. I pulled my sweater closer around me. I was shivering now. *How I longed to see the sun, to feel its warmth on my body again.* I was tired of this darkness, and all that it was hiding.

I didn't know how long I had been walking, but it felt like an eternity. I was getting desperate. No matter how much I searched, I couldn't find her. I had to get help. I couldn't do this alone. If I went back now, I could call the police. Aizawa would help me for sure. I didn't want to leave my daughter, but what choice did I have?

That's what I kept telling myself as I headed back toward the river. As the sound of water grew louder and louder, I couldn't help but feel that guilt tearing into my heart. Maybe only a mother could understand that pain. But there was no other way. I was determined now. Somewhere deep inside of me, I had made up my mind. The river was so close now. I knew it wouldn't be long.

"Hang on, Suzu," I whispered to the forest. "Mama's going to get help. I'm going to find you. I promise."

By the time I reached the entrance, night had fallen, and I could barely see in front of me. It was so strange. There were no stars to guide me, no moon even. Just the darkness, as if I had never left the forest. It didn't matter. I had found my way back in the night many times before. This time would be no different.

I just had to cross the bridge. Once I reached the other side, I could follow the river home. And in no time, I would be holding Suzu in my arms again. I forced myself to believe it, even if all I felt in my heart was doubt. I steeled myself against my grief. I told myself again that this was the only way. But just as I was about to take a step forward, I could feel the cold air off the river push up from below. A cry caught in my throat. I scrambled back onto the ledge, trying to catch my breath. *What was happening? I was just here. I couldn't have been in the forest that long.* But no matter how much I tried to convince myself, I couldn't deny what had just happened. I sat up on the ledge and looked across the river to Kasumi-machi. Even in that darkness, I knew the truth. I would never get back now.

The bridge was gone.

- 14 -

THE FOG BEGAN TO ROLL IN ACROSS THE RIVER. The rain was coming. I could feel it. But I didn't know if I could go back into the pine forest. I was afraid of that darkness. It felt like being swallowed in a grief so deep that I'd never be able to escape. I told myself that I'd wait until the sky would clear, until I could see the stars once more. I needed that little bit of light. I needed something to hold onto.

The pine trees began to grow blurry. I wiped my eyes on my sleeve and forced myself to think. I was trapped. There was no way home without the bridge. My daughter was lost somewhere in that dark forest, and there was nothing I could do to save her, nothing I could do to help. It would be at least morning before I could even begin to search for her again.

Deep down, I could feel that sense of hope slipping away. I was desperate already. I didn't know what to do. I didn't know how to help her. It took everything inside of me to hold on, to not let go, to not jump off that ledge. Just when I was about to give up, I felt something soft brush against my cheek. It was floating down from the sky, one after another, until it was snowing all around me.

I held out my hand, and something small and delicate settled into my palm. Its scent began to fill the air, reaching out and winding itself around me like a gentle embrace. *Peach blossoms.* It was the fragrance of that tea and the wagashi. It was the way I had felt in that garden room in my father's house. All at once, my heart hurt, and I couldn't stop crying.

"Akane? Is that you?" I whispered. I searched the night. "Akane!" I screamed. But no one answered me. Not a soul was there, but I couldn't deny it. Something, somewhere was calling me in.

I stood up, and once again turned back to the forest. I could hear my heart pounding in my ears. It was so loud now that the sound of the river began to fade away. Maybe I was just fooling myself. Maybe it wasn't a sign after all. But I couldn't just sit there anymore. I had to do something, anything to find my daughter.

I took a step forward and then another and another. Before I knew it, I was completely engulfed in that darkness again. The scent of peach blossoms was still in the air, but even that fragrance began to grow faint. I turned to look back. The branches had already covered the entrance. There was no turning back now.

Little by little, a strange quiet settled all around me. I couldn't hear anything anymore. Not the river, nor the rustle of leaves above me. Everything was muted, as if I had suddenly plunged underwater again. I stopped. I closed my eyes. I tried to listen as hard as I could, but it was useless.

And then, in that stillness, it arrived. Even though I couldn't see her, she sounded close, like she was standing right here next to me.

"Suzu!" I cried. "Suzu!" I was shouting at the top of my lungs, but no sound came out of my mouth. *Why couldn't I make her hear me? What was happening?* I was frantic. Her voice was getting louder and louder. My daughter was crying, but I couldn't help her at all.

"Mama! Where are you?"

"I'm here!" I cried. "Suzu!" My eyes desperately searched the forest. But no matter how hard I tried, I couldn't see through the darkness. I was breaking under the weight of my grief. She had to be here somewhere. She just had to be. Her voice was so clear. I could hear her. She was singing now. My daughter was singing that song my mother used to sing to me as a child. It slipped inside my heart, squeezing it so tightly, I could hardly breathe. I felt like I was going crazy. I missed them both so much.

"Suzu!" More than anything else, I wanted to see her. I wanted to hold her in my arms again. There was no way that I could go on living without her. *Didn't the gods know?* I had already lost Naoki. To lose my daughter was like losing him all over again. I collapsed to the ground, wailing with grief. If someone had heard me, they would have thought the whole forest was weeping.

But it was just me, an ordinary woman, a widow, a mother, who had already lost too much and wondered how much more she could stand to have taken away from her. My sadness was unbearable. Any hope I had felt earlier had left me, and now I felt helpless to change my situation at all.

I didn't know how long I sat there on the forest floor, my hands dirty and my face stained with tears. But I couldn't stop crying. It was as if I had already lost Suzu. I thought I'd die if I couldn't see my daughter again. Those thoughts turned over and over in my head, but I just couldn't understand it. It didn't make sense. Why was this happening to us?

"How much are you going to take from me?" I yelled to the gods. "You already have my mother and my husband. I won't let you take my daughter too!"

I was so consumed with grief that I hadn't noticed the pool of light forming around me. All of a sudden, I looked up and through a large opening in the canopy, it was the moon. For a moment there, I let that light soak into my skin. I wanted it to wash away the darkness I carried inside. I wanted to shine again, so that when I saw Naoki at the end of my life, he would recognize me immediately.

In the moonlight, I was a child again. It was not long after my mother had left. Before I hated my father. Before I was afraid of the darkness. On those nights when I couldn't sleep, when I couldn't contain my grief inside of me, I'd stay on the engawa and let the moon embrace me in her light.

"Mama," I would whisper. "When are you coming home?" But the moon never answered me. *How could it?* It was too far away. Even then, I had hoped it would hear me. I hoped it would tell me what to do.

All that time, I never knew that my father was watching me. From where he stood, the moonlight had illuminated my whole being. If I had seen him then, I would have seen how much I had broken his heart. Tears pooled in his eyes.

"Nami." That was all he said, my name. But I didn't hear him.

How I missed that Papa! After Mama left, that man slowly disappeared from my life, until I couldn't recognize him anymore. Maybe I never remembered the good times because it hurt too much to remember that he had once cared about me, that he had once loved me. It was too hard to hope that those times would ever come back again.

Maybe if my father had died right after Mama had left, when his heart was still tender, I would have wanted to say goodbye. I would have seen how cold and stiff his body was. I would have taken off my own scarf and put it around his shoulders and chest to keep him warm.

Back then, I was too young to really know what was going on. But I remembered my father's face. I felt his pain. I knew what sadness looked like even at that young age. I couldn't understand why he had retreated, why he had moved into a hard shell that not even I, his daughter, had access to. All I knew was, how I was losing someone inch by inch. Then how I lost him. And no matter what I did, I could never get him back.

After that incident with the girl in my class, I saw my father sitting by himself in the garden. It was late in the night, when he thought that I had already gone to bed. But I was up. I saw him weeping. I could hear him from my room. I slowly slid the shoji door open, just a little, just enough, so that I could see him. He was sitting on my mother's bench, his head in his hands.

"Sanae, I don't know how to take care of her. Nami is so young. I don't know how to love her when she's all I have left of you. Sanae. Sanae, I'm so sorry." He kept apologizing to her, even though she was gone.

I couldn't take this sadness. It was so heavy that I was dying under its weight. No matter what I did, I couldn't stop it. One after another, the memories rained down on me, this flood of grief. But he didn't deserve my tears. I didn't want to cry over my father. I would never forgive him, not even if my life depended on it. But it was like I couldn't control it. The sadness had already taken over my whole being.

All of a sudden, he emerged from the shadows. His fur was almost luminous in the light. I had missed that thick white coat. Years had passed, but I remembered the dog. Even now, sitting there in front of me, he was so big, almost wolf-like in the bright moonlight. But this time, he didn't welcome me. He growled, baring his teeth. I scrambled back against a tree, but he kept barking.

My heart was pounding. I sank down into a ball and covered my ears. I waited for the attack. I felt him move closer to me, his barking growing louder and louder. I don't know how long it lasted, but slowly, I could feel that heaviness lift. The memories were beginning to fade. My daughter's voice quieted to a murmur, and then it was gone. The nostalgia that had rushed at me like a wave had finally pulled away. And the moon, who had bathed me in its light, left me in the darkness once again.

The Akita licked my face. I sat up and hugged him with all my might. I buried my face in that pure white fur. The dog hadn't been barking at me. He didn't think I was a fox. He was trying to save me from my sadness. I wanted to thank him. I wanted to look into his eyes again and know that he was real.

But he was already moving forward.

- 15 -

THE AKITA WALKED A COUPLE OF PACES IN FRONT OF ME. His footsteps were so quiet, it was hard to believe that he was real. Even in the shadows, his coat seemed to glow the blue-white of a star. Whenever he'd stop for me, I found myself reaching out and touching his fur, just to know that he was really there, just to believe that this wasn't a dream.

I didn't know where he was taking me, but he was my only guide, my only way home. *What choice did I have?* When he stopped, I stopped. When he started up again, so did I. No matter how lost I felt, the thought of being left by myself was too much to bear. I didn't want to be alone in this darkness again. But it was inevitable that I would fall behind.

"Take him." The man put the leash in my father's hand and met his gaze with a hard stare. "He'll protect you." My father looked at the dog. His dark brown coat was dull and speckled with white. His tail wagged eagerly. But I knew my father felt torn.

The talk had already started. *My mother had run away with another man. She was a fox.* That's what they said. By that time, too many weeks had passed to even hope that they were wrong. But the man understood. My father couldn't give up now. Once he did, my mother would be a fox in their eyes forever, and there was no need to search for a woman like that. They would never find her.

My father stared at the leash in his hand. I didn't want him to believe that man. Mama wasn't a fox. From the bottom of my heart, I knew she loved him. There was no reason for her to run away with someone else. *Didn't he know that?*

"Don't worry about me," he said, as he returned the leash to the man. "I'll be okay." When he said it, I felt a sense of relief wash over me. No matter what had happened, no matter what my father hadn't understood, he still believed in my mother.

The man shook his head. "You have to take him, Isao. Only a dog knows if a woman is really a fox." He held out the leash to him again, shaking it, as if to emphasize how serious the matter was. I could see the desperation in the man's face.

"Sanae wasn't a fox. She was happy here."

"You don't understand. You can never trust a fox. You won't know who they really are or what they really want."

I wouldn't believe him. The fox had been my friend. She had come to me in the night when there was no one else to comfort me, no one else to carry my grief. No matter what he said, I wasn't going to betray her. Still, the pine forest was off limits. It wasn't because I was afraid of disappointing my father or fearful of what he might do if he found out. I stayed away, because I could never bring myself to cross that bridge.

After all that had happened, how could I?

My father stood there for a long time with the leash in his hand. If he took the dog now, it was like he was saying that he believed my mother was a fox, and he didn't want to. Deep down, I knew that he wanted to search the forest by himself. He would have welcomed a fox or a ghost, even. At that point, he was desperate to find something, anything to keep going, anything to keep him from losing hope.

In the end, I wondered why my father had listened to the man that day. If he had gone into that forest alone, would that wave of nostalgia crash over him like it did me? I couldn't be sure. All I knew was, I couldn't control it.

When the wave came, it drowned me in those memories. I was held under by that grief until I couldn't breathe. Even the sweetest times became too much for me to hold onto. Honestly, I don't know what I would have done if the Akita hadn't shown up.

The darkness seemed endless. I didn't know how long we had been walking, but it felt like we would never escape it. I was tired. My feet were aching, but I couldn't stop. If I were ever going to get out of here and find Suzu, the only chance I had was with the Akita.

Little by little, the forest began to thin. The old pines gave way to cedar trees again, and the night that had once felt eternal began to fade with the coming dawn. When I looked up, I could see a small patch of blue appear in the morning sky. Just the sight of it made me hopeful. I told myself that we were going to find my daughter. I held onto that wish with all my heart.

Up ahead, the Akita stopped. His ears perked up, and he began to sniff the air. I followed his gaze, but whatever he was sensing was lost on me. There was only the forest and that small patch of blue sky, nothing else. When I turned to look back, I couldn't even see where the forest began anymore. And the sound of water had gone completely silent. We were so far from Kasumi-machi now that the thought of returning home felt next to impossible.

The Akita started up again. He was moving faster now, as if he wanted me to hurry. I wondered where we were going. We had been walking forever. At that point, all I wanted to do was rest. My heart was weary. My body was sore. I didn't think I could bear this journey much longer.

All of a sudden, the fog began to roll in like a wave. The air became sharp and biting. I shivered. I pulled my sweater tighter around me, but it didn't help. I was so cold that my body hurt. I waited for the snow, but it never came. Here, the fog ruled. It covered everything. I could barely see the edge of the forest now.

The clouds began to cluster around me as if I were one of the trees. There was no way I was going to go on, not when I couldn't see two feet in front of me. But the fog was moving, and soon it thinned into smoke. In that brief clearing, I saw it, a flash of vermillion. I shook my head. I didn't know what was real anymore. In this forest, I just couldn't be sure. But when I looked again, there it was, solitary and majestic among the cedars.

Before I knew it, I was standing beside a large red torii. It was so tall that it seemed to reach all the way to the sky. But there wasn't just that one gate. There must've been hundreds, maybe even thousands of those red gates, one after the other, winding up into the clouds. I couldn't believe it. Up until now, all I had seen was the forest and the never-ending darkness. But this was like something almost mythical.

I looked around for the Akita, but he had disappeared. I had taken my eyes off of him for just a moment, and now, I was alone again. My chest tightened with fear. I turned to look behind me. We had come too far to turn back. In fact, the river, the canopy of trees and even the forest path had vanished behind the clouds. Tears filled my eyes.

I didn't know if I could go on. I didn't even know where I was anymore. *How was I supposed to find my daughter now?* The silence in that fog was making me crazy. Was I just hearing things? But then, I heard it again. Her laughter. Suzu was laughing. I looked around frantically, trying to find where she was.

"Suzu! Suzu! Where are you?" Her voice echoed in my ears as the fog continued to close in around me. I tried to push forward. I was desperate now. I had to see her. I needed to know that she was okay.

All at once, she appeared in front of me. My daughter was laughing. It felt like I hadn't heard her laugh for so long. I couldn't believe it. *Was this even real?* It didn't matter. In an instant, she ran ahead without me.

"Suzu!" I cried. Without even realizing it, I followed her through the first torii and then the second and the third. With each gate, the trail was beginning to ascend. The fog was shifting. I tried not to lose her, but she kept moving in and out of my sight. The air was getting colder. It was getting harder and harder for me to breathe. I wished that she would stop for a moment. I wanted to hold her in my arms. I wanted to be sure that what I was seeing was really my daughter and not a ghost. But she wouldn't stop.

I climbed higher and higher, passing through each of the red gates. The pathway wound up and up, but to where, I just couldn't tell. I kept walking. I couldn't see the blue sky anymore. Everything had turned white. I was determined not to lose her. I gathered whatever courage I had left. No matter what, I knew I couldn't give up.

When the fog broke again, Suzu was there, waving at me. "Mama!" she cried. She was smiling. She was so high up on the mountain now, it almost looked as though she were standing on the clouds. I felt a sense of relief wash over me. I was so happy that I ran ahead. It wouldn't be long before we'd be together. But the fog closed in. It wrapped itself around me like a blindfold. Suzu had to be in front of me. I just saw her there. I took a step forward. But I was mistaken.

All of a sudden, the ground beneath me began to give way. I was falling. The wind pushed up against me, its sound like a jet engine. Soon, I was dropping faster and faster, until the darkness consumed me whole. I felt it inside. It had already soaked into every part of my being. I told myself that this was only a dream. I was going to wake up. I had to wake up. *Didn't the gods know?* I was too young to die. I didn't want to die.

Suzu!

- 16 -

SOMETHING WET LICKED MY FACE. When I opened my eyes, the Akita was standing on all fours, looking down at me. Even in that darkness, I could see the ice blue of his eyes. I tried to get up. I wanted to hold him. I wanted to bury my face in his thick white fur, but my body ached all over. I tasted blood in my mouth, a raw, rusty concoction that made me want to throw up. But I was almost grateful for it. It was the only thing real, the only thing that made me believe that I was still alive.

The Akita lay down next to me. His head rested on his paws, but his gaze was focused on somewhere beyond. I didn't know what he was waiting for. I couldn't see it in the darkness. I couldn't make out where I had ended up. All I knew was, the ground was solid beneath me. Night had fallen. Up above, the black sky stretched for miles, the stars, the only light. I waited for the night to fade into day. It was all I could do. *The dawn had to come at some point, didn't it?* I wanted to see the sun again. I wanted to feel that warmth on my skin. But I couldn't wait any longer. I was too tired. And before I knew it, I had closed my eyes.

I was descending into the darkness. I couldn't see it, but I felt the wind push up against me. I was falling. My body was dropping faster and faster inside this endless abyss. I kept waiting for the crash, for my bones to shatter into pieces, but it never came. And no matter what I did, I couldn't escape the sadness. There was no one there to help me, and soon, I was drowning in the night.

I wanted to let go. I wanted to let everything end. It was too hard to hold on, to keep my head above water. All of a sudden, my mother's voice broke through the gloom. Even though it had been years, I had never forgotten that sound. Tears rolled down my cheeks. She was singing that song, the one she always sang. All at once, a small voice began to sing along with her. It was my daughter. In that moment, my heart ached. I couldn't bear it. I missed them both so much. Then their voices faded, and the world fell silent once again.

I didn't know how much time had passed. I must have fallen asleep at least once or twice. At that point, I wasn't sure anymore. I wasn't even certain if I were still awake. No matter how many times I opened my eyes, the sky was still the same. I wanted time to move. I wanted the dawn to find me, but in a place like this one, it seemed like it would always be night, like the stars wouldn't shift at all.

Finally, the pain began to fade away. I could feel my body grow lighter. I sat up and looked out into the distance. There was just starlight here. Not even the moon graced this sky. Even when my eyes adjusted to the darkness, I couldn't really see anything.

Nothing living seemed to exist here except for me and maybe the Akita. In my mind, I wondered where my daughter was. How could she survive the night alone in a place like this? The thought of her being gone pierced my heart. Even now, I couldn't understand it. I saw her as clear as day in the clouds. *But where did she go? Had she already joined Naoki?*

The Akita sat up. He must've known that I was here, that I was sitting right beside him, but he didn't look at me. Instead, he stared far out into the night. It was clear that he was waiting for someone or something to arrive. After a while, he lay back down again and rested his head on his paws. But he didn't sleep. His eyes continued to scan the dark plain. His ears stayed perked up. Whatever he was listening for, I didn't really know. I couldn't hear anything.

I reached out and touched his fur. I wanted him to see me then, to look into my eyes. I hoped that if he stared at me long enough, I would know where I was and why I was here. I wished that he could give me answers to my questions. Then I would know for sure what had really happened. I would know if I were really dead. But it didn't matter. Even if he met my gaze, he was still listening to someone else far far away.

All of a sudden, the Akita stood up and sniffed the air. Whatever he was waiting for had arrived. He began to follow the scent. He didn't look back. Deep down, I knew he didn't want me to come with him. But I got up. I wasn't going to be left behind. I tried to rush after him, but he moved too fast for me. Then, he broke into a run. I tried to keep up. But I was no match for a wolf's kin.

I stood there, breathless, not knowing what to do next. I peered out to where the Akita had gone. There were no mountains here, no silhouettes of trees or even houses. I was in some kind of flat land or desert where the vast expanse of sky seemed to wrap around this part of the earth or wherever this was. I was lost in this dark world, and the only creature that knew the way back had left. I dropped to the ground and began to cry. The thought of never seeing Suzu and Bachan again made my heart hurt.

I closed my eyes. But this time, I wouldn't fall sleep. The thunder was in the earth, filling the desert like a storm. It was approaching fast. I got up quickly and looked out to where the Akita had run. But I couldn't see anything. The sound grew louder. It vibrated in my chest, filling my whole body with its urgency.

Then, the storm broke. I could hear the clapping of hooves on the desert floor. It was racing toward me, but there was nowhere to hide. In that moment, I prayed that I would wake up, that any minute now, I would open my eyes, and this would all be a bad dream. But I knew better.

All at once, the thunder stopped, and I could hear a horse breathing heavily not far from where I stood. There were bells on its reins. In my heart, they felt like an alarm. The rider got off and stepped closer to me. In the faint starlight, I could make out his silhouette.

The man was a giant, even on the ground. He looked even bigger with his dark cape billowing behind him like a sail. I could smell blood in the air. I wondered if he had ever taken a life, if he had ever killed a man with his bare hands. He must have. He felt like a true warrior, someone ready to fight the enemy or die trying. But I understood from his presence that he was no ordinary fighter.

This man felt more like a god.

- 17 -

THERE WAS NO QUESTION THAT THE MAN BELONGED to the night. His body, his cape, even his horse seemed to melt into the murky darkness. When the Akita peered out from behind him, his snow-white fur was such a contrast, that he actually glowed. I wanted to run to him then. I wanted to hold the Akita in my arms. But the man had already claimed him.

He knelt down and buried his face in the dog's thick white fur. The loyalties were unfolding before me, and all I could do was watch. In that moment, I would have given anything to trade places with the man. I missed the Akita so badly, I almost cried. But there was no time for tears. Even in the shadows, I could feel the man watching me.

All of a sudden, he stood up. The man became a giant again. I tried to back away, but I couldn't move. As he inched closer to me, I could see his eyes. They were shining like the moonlight. The man met my gaze. I wanted to turn away, but he held my face in his hands. He made me look at him. In that moment, my heart was pounding so loud that I couldn't hear anything else. I wanted to scream, but who would hear me? Who would save me in this darkness?

Then I felt it. My eyes began to burn. It was a pain so unbearable, I thought I was going to die. I was sobbing now, but I couldn't look away. I couldn't close my eyes. The man's eyes were locked onto mine. If this were some kind of test, I knew that I couldn't back down. I couldn't just give up. I had to be strong, or I would never see my daughter again. But I didn't know how much more of this I could take.

After what seemed like forever, he let me go, and I fell hard to the ground. When I looked up again, the night had become darker. The stars had disappeared. Everything was quiet except for the sound of the man's cape blowing in the wind. I looked for him in the night, but I couldn't see anything anymore. I wondered what he wanted with me. *What good would I be to him blind?* I braced myself for the worst. I waited for his next move. But he just stood there, silent. Then the Akita started barking.

The man got on his horse. "Get on!" he ordered. His voice was strong, like it had commanded a thousand men to charge an enemy. I stood up. He grabbed for my hand, but I pulled it away.

"Where are you taking me?"

"There's no time! Get on!" I wanted to refuse him. I wanted to keep my two feet on the ground, until I knew where we were going. But what choice did I have? I didn't want to be abandoned in the night. I had to trust him. He was my only guide.

I held out my hand, and he pulled me onto his horse in one fluid motion. In no time, we were racing across the desert. I could feel his breath on my shoulder. I could hear the urgency in his voice. I had no idea where we were headed, but the man pushed his horse onward as if our lives depended on it. Then, in the distance, I could feel it. The darkness was beginning to lift.

"Don't get excited," the man said to me. "The light isn't a good thing here. It signals that there's a human. We must get to her before it gets any brighter."

"Her?"

"The sun. Close your eyes," he said to me.

"I can't see anything anyway."

"It doesn't matter. This kind of brightness will blind you forever."

After a while, his horse slowed down to a trot and finally came to a stop. I felt a rush of wind hit my face. I heard his voice echo. We must have been at the edge of some sort of deep cavern. The man got off and put the reins in my hands. I heard his footsteps travel away from me and then leap down into the abyss. Moments later, everything went dark again.

"What did you do?" I asked him when he returned.

"A little bit of magic. It should fool her for a couple of days. Enough time to get you back." *Get me back? Get me back where? Where was this place?* I wanted to ask him so many questions, but there was no time for him to explain. He had already mounted his horse behind me, and we were riding off again into the night.

We traveled for hours in the darkness. All that time, it felt like a dream. I was going in and out of sleep to the rhythm of his horse, and after a while, I couldn't tell if I were awake or still sleeping. I wanted to ask him where he was taking me. There had to be a destination. There had to be a reason why I was here. But I had to admit, a part of me didn't want to know. I was afraid he'd tell me this whole thing was a lie, and after all that I had been through, I didn't want my suffering to be for nothing. Maybe not knowing was better than getting the answer you didn't want. Maybe that's why I didn't say anything.

All of a sudden, we started to descend. The air around me began to grow warmer, and I could hear a fire crackling in the background. The man dismounted and pulled me off his horse. He guided me to sit down. Soon, I could feel the Akita brush up against my leg. I held him in my arms and buried my face in his fur. I missed him so much, even though, he had been there all along.

When I looked up again, the room was slowly growing brighter. I could see colors and shapes beginning to form right in front of me. The more I blinked away the darkness, the clearer my sight became, and moments later, I could see the ice blue eyes of the Akita staring back at me.

We were inside what looked like an underground cave. A fire had been made, its orange flames casting tall shadows against the stone. If it weren't for the Akita, I would have felt trapped in the belly of the earth. But his warmth calmed me, made me feel whole. The man was at the fire, roasting meat. He broke the bread himself. When he finished, he set the food down in front of me.

"You have to eat," he said to me. But I shook my head. Even after all this time, I wasn't hungry. "It's not only for you."

"What?"

"Nothing. It's just that you'll never make it on this journey if you don't eat. We have a long way to go." I looked up at him then, sitting across from me.

All this time, I hadn't seen his face. I had only heard the urgency of his voice. But now, by the light of the fire, I saw him for the first time. He was older than me, maybe ten years or more, dressed in full samurai battle gear. His face was hard, weathered a little. He had a strong nose, as if he were part European or some other nationality besides Japanese. As he sat there before me, he didn't look like a god anymore. His eyes were human again, gentle brown eyes that glowed by the light of the flame. They were kind eyes, but there was also a hardness that lived there, something closed off, something not permitted. Still, those eyes made me want to ask him all that was in my heart.

"Why did you save me?" The man didn't give me an answer right away. In fact, he took his time with the Akita. He stroked the dog's fur and fed him a piece of meat.

"What do you mean?"

"You said you'd give me three days."

He stopped then and stared hard into my eyes. "It takes at least three days to take you back."

"Take me back where?"

"To where you came from."

My heart sank. I didn't want to go back. "I'm not going back. Not without my daughter."

"How do you know she's even here?"

"She has to be. She was at the top of that mountain. I saw her with my own eyes."

"How can you be so sure?"

I stared at him then. "I know what I saw. I know she led me here. I have to find her."

"Look, you're not supposed to be here. Luckily, you only made it this far. The deeper you go, the harder it is to return. I can get you back without any consequences, but you'll have to listen to me."

"Where is here?" The man looked directly into my eyes. He had a stare that warned me that he could blind me again at any time.

"This is the Eternal Night. Everyone must pass through here to get somewhere else." I turned the man's words over and over in my head.

"Does that mean I'm dead?" The man didn't answer me. In his silence, I knew. I was in the underworld. Somehow, my daughter had led me here. And right now, there was only one reason I could think of as to why she would do that.

"Is my husband here?" I asked. But the man wouldn't answer me. "If everyone must pass through here, then you must have seen him."

The man averted his gaze. "You're mistaken," he said, but by that time, I didn't believe him.

"I can't leave," I told him finally. "I won't leave. Not until I see him with my own eyes."

"Don't you get it? You're not supposed to be here. You're human. That's why I blinded you. The more you see, the more it's unlikely that you'll be able to return." He stood up then. "Do you want that?" I knew he was frustrated with me, but I wouldn't back down. Not now.

"I don't care."

"Are you telling me that you don't want to see your daughter again? Or live your life? Are you willing to give that up for just a glimpse of the dead?"

Deep down, I knew he was right, but I couldn't help myself. He didn't know how much I missed Naoki. I needed to feel his arms around me again. I needed him to tell me why he died, why he was there at the bridge. I didn't think I could go on living if I didn't know.

I was crying now, begging him to change his mind. "Just let me see him. Even just once would be enough." I don't know why I said it, but for a split second, I swear his expression softened. I couldn't explain it, but I felt like my words had gotten through to him.

But no matter how much I pleaded, he wouldn't tell me what I wanted to hear. I stood up then. I didn't know where I would go or what I would do, but I knew I had to leave now. I had to find Naoki. He had to be here, somewhere in the Eternal Night.

In that moment, the man lunged forward and grabbed me by the arms. His voice got loud. "There are rules here in the Eternal Night. They are finite. I cannot go against them." I stared into his eyes. The way he looked at me made me want to be held by him. I could see the pain that lived there.

He touched my cheek. There was a war going on inside his heart.

"Then why did my daughter lead me here?" He let go of me and sat back down. He wouldn't look at me then. Deep down, he didn't know how to answer me.

"You shouldn't have followed her."

"But she's my daughter. I wasn't about to lose her too. Wasn't it enough for me to lose my husband? Plus, it was like she wanted me to follow her. I can't explain it."

"But maybe it wasn't for the reason you think. Maybe it had nothing to do with your husband at all." He wouldn't look at me. It was clear that he had already said too much.

"Why did you save me then?" I cried. "You should've left me out there in that desert night. It would have been easier than living through the hell I've been through. Do you know what it's like to lose your husband at an age when your lives are supposed to be just beginning? Do you know what it's like to have him taken from you in a flash, to not even get a chance to say goodbye? Do you? When Suzu was born, I could be a mother because Naoki was there. He was teaching me how to love again. But since he died, I don't know how to be a good mother to my daughter. And now she's suffering because of me."

"You know how to be a good mother. You know how to love. You just have to remember."

"But I don't even remember what it was like to be embraced by my own mother. I don't know what it's like to let someone into my whole heart. And if I can't remember, then how am I supposed to truly love my own child? I don't want my daughter to become a fox daughter like how I was. But right now, I don't see how I can avoid it."

I looked up at the man then. His face was still strong, but his eyes were sad, and his voice had grown weary. That expression on his face—he looked like he wanted to take me into his arms, like he wanted to comfort me. But he couldn't.

"You're not a fox daughter," he said finally.

"How do you know? You weren't there when Mama disappeared, when the townspeople whispered behind our backs." I couldn't take it. My heart was so overwhelmed with memories that I began to weep. "You weren't there when my father—" I couldn't continue.

The man didn't answer me. He may have been a god, but he didn't have all the answers. He didn't know everything. The war raged on in his heart. But for the moment, all he could do was look on.

No matter what I said, no matter how much I may have moved his heart, the man was going to take me home. We would leave this darkness. We would descend onto that winding pathway of red torii, through the fog and shadows, the pine forest, until we once again reached the bridge, the river, and my life in Kasumi-machi.

I should have been grateful to him. After all, the worst thing was to be left behind in the night. But if I were right, if Naoki and Suzu were really somewhere in the Eternal Night, I knew that I couldn't return yet. I didn't want to. My world was here, with them. But I didn't know how to convince the man.

Since we left the cave, he hadn't said a word to me. It was probably better that way. Every answer that came out of his mouth just led to more and more questions in my mind; questions he couldn't or wouldn't give me the answers to. But it was so strange. Even now, I couldn't be mad at him.

When I slept in his arms, I felt his warmth surround me, and even if I couldn't see him, I couldn't forget the way he looked at me in the cave. It was the same look that Naoki had given me that first day at the river, and the time we left my father's house and when I tried to leave the inn. That wave of nostalgia washed over me. It soaked every cell in my body, until I was carrying the ocean within me—all those tears, all that grief, all that love.

From the bottom of my heart, I knew that the man wasn't an unfeeling being. He may have been some god of the underworld, but the way he looked at me, showed me that he could feel my sorrows. He could feel my pain. But in the end, he was at the mercy of what was right in his world, no matter how much it hurt me.

We continued on in silence. I didn't know how long we had been riding. The Eternal Night was so large, so vast that I couldn't even imagine when we would reach its edge. The man had told me that all souls must past through here in order to move on to somewhere else. I wish I would have known that before he blinded me. Then I would have searched hard for Naoki, Suzu, or even my mother. But now, it felt like I would only see her in my dreams.

"A mother's embrace is like a vow," he whispered.

I opened my eyes. Even though my world was still in darkness, his voice filled me with hope again. More than ever, I wished for the dawn. I wanted to see his face. I wanted to know exactly what he was feeling. All I had in the night was the sound of his words and the feel of his heart pounding hard against my back. It was a strong heart, much stronger than my own. His was a heart that had loved many people.

He didn't say anything after that. Maybe he hadn't wanted me to hear him. Maybe he thought that I was sleeping. I placed my hand over his. I wanted him to know that I was listening.

"I did have a mother once," he continued. "I was human, after all. My mother brought me into this world, but she died when I was very young, as did my father."

"How did they die?" The words flew out of my mouth before I had time to think. I couldn't hold onto them. A part of me had to know. "I'm sorry. That was thoughtless of me."

"A fire. It was an accident, but I was careless." My face grew hot with tears. In that moment, I felt like he was the only person in the world who could understand me, the only one who could make sense of my heart. "I was lucky though."

"How can you say that? You lost your parents."

He paused for a moment as if he were remembering them. "Not long after they died, I was adopted into a warrior family. Eventually, I was given the duty of protecting a court lady's daughter, and I did. In time, she became my family." I didn't have to see his face to know that he was smiling.

"You loved her, didn't you?"

"I gave my life for her."

"Your life?"

"Yes. Because that was my vow."

"I don't understand."

"When I couldn't save my parents in the fire, I felt a deep sense of guilt, so much so that my heart hardened over time. I needed a way to redeem myself, or I would never move on. She was my second chance. In honor of my parents, I vowed that I would protect her in that life and after I died, every life thereafter, for an eternity."

"You made a promise like that?" In that moment, my love for Naoki seemed so small in comparison.

"Of course."

"How?"

"From a place of great love." He paused for moment.

"What is it?" It felt like he wanted to tell me something more, but I knew that he was holding back.

"It's nothing."

We rode on in silence for a long time. In that quiet, I thought about Naoki and what we had promised each other when we got married. We would love, honor, and cherish each other until death do us part. *But over lifetimes? For an eternity?* He didn't promise me that, nor did I. *And my mother? Had she ever made such a vow?* I was certain that she made one to my father when she married him. But did she make one for me? Did she promise me anything?

"So, I guess it feels like that," the man said all of a sudden.

"What?"

"A mother's embrace. It feels like a vow, something made with great love." The man brought his arms around me for a moment. I leaned back into his chest as if it were the most natural thing in the world.

"But I don't remember what it felt like. I know Mama came in a dream once. I can see myself in her arms, but I don't remember the feeling."

"Even if you don't remember, I'm certain that she embraced you many times. Deep inside her heart, she didn't want to leave you."

"How do you know?" The man didn't say anything. "Please!" I cried. "You must know something." My cheeks burned with tears. I felt so desperate already. "If everyone passes through the Eternal Night, you must have seen her," I sobbed.

The man held me tightly in his arms. He let me cry until the sea had left me again. Then, I heard his voice, a mere whisper next to my ear. "I don't know anything about your mother. I can only imagine what a mother would do. And I can tell you that most mothers do not abandon their children willingly."

But that day, my mother disappeared on the bridge. I heard her geta walking away from me. *Didn't he understand?* If she had been a good mother, would she have left me behind? Would she have left me with my father? Until Naoki, there was no one there to protect me.

"Nobody makes vows like that in real life," I said to him after a while. "You know, saving someone." I could hear that hard edge return to my voice. *How I envied that court lady's daughter!* To have someone vow to protect you was the stuff of fairy tales.

"Protecting someone and saving them are two different things." He was careful with his words. Maybe if Naoki were here, he would have disagreed.

I turned to him, even though I couldn't see his face. "What do you mean?"

"As a guardian of the underworld, I couldn't save her. I cannot interfere with human choices, no matter how much it may hurt me."

"Then how did you protect her?"

"I protected her heart."

As soon as he said it, the darkness began to lift. I could see his eyes again, those soft, brown eyes looking straight into mine. All around us, it was still night, but the landscape had completely changed. I could smell the pine trees in the air. My heart sank. We were in the pine forest again. Before I knew it, we would be at that bridge, and I'd have to figure out how to live without those missing pieces of my heart. I didn't want to go back. There was so much more that I needed the man to say. But I knew he wouldn't listen.

The man got off his horse and helped me down. If this were really Kasumi-machi, it should've been summer. In fact, the rainy season would have just ended. The air would have been filled with moisture and the ground, muddy. But when I looked down, there was snow beneath my feet; a first snow, soft, powdery, and white. I couldn't understand it. *Didn't he say that he was going to take me back?*

But there was no time to ask him anything. He was already walking away from me. I ran to catch up with him.

Together, we were heading for a clearing in the pines. I could see the light, and all at once, I wanted to be enveloped in that warm orange glow of home. We weren't in the Eternal Night anymore. We definitely weren't in Kasumi-machi. Wherever this place was, the stars were alive.

I stood in the middle of that snowfield like a dream. At least, it felt that way. All around me, there must have been thousands of stars on the snow, each one waiting for us like glowing cocoons. I was mesmerized. None of it felt real, yet I couldn't shake the feeling that I had been here before, even though I knew it was impossible.

When I looked up at the man, his gaze was fixed to the night sky. Several stars shot across the darkness and fell to the snow. All I could do was stand there and watch in awe.

Even the stars above gave off that warmth, that feeling I had when I was with someone I loved. I couldn't explain it. I just wanted to catch a star in my hands and place it in my heart for safekeeping. I was sure a light like that would be enough to make it grow.

"Do you know what shooting stars really are?" the man asked me. His expression was almost nostalgic now.

"No, I don't."

"They're souls, souls that come back down to earth." The man smiled at me. It was the first time I had ever seen him smile like that.

"Where are we?" I asked. He met my eyes again. I didn't expect him to tell me. There were rules. But I really wanted to know.

"Where good people are reborn."

In that moment, a single star fell from the sky. It didn't burn across the night in a fiery blaze. Instead, this one seemed to float down like a piece of confetti or a delicate flower petal. Before my eyes, its light grew bigger and bigger, until all of a sudden, I could hear it, the soft tinkling of a tiny bell. There were footprints in the snow. Someone was definitely walking toward us, but I couldn't make out who it was. Then slowly in the glowing starlight, it began to appear in the distance like a mirage.

It was a young woman, not much older than me. She was dressed in a pink yukata with yellow flowers, and she held a red umbrella to keep away the snow. I looked back at the man. *It was true, wasn't it?* He smiled at me and nodded. I waited for her to come closer; my heart pounding so hard I thought I would faint. I was afraid to even blink, thinking that if I did, everything before me would disappear, and I didn't want that, not after I had waited so long. I couldn't believe it. In my heart, I must have imagined this scene a million times.

But not once did it ever look like this.

- 19 -

I TOLD MYSELF THAT I WASN'T LOOKING, but the truth is, I never stopped. Whenever passengers got off the train, I found myself searching for her in every woman's face. All this time, I wanted to believe that I would see her, that maybe one day, the crowd would thin, and she would be standing right there waiting for me.

She would be wearing that pink yukata, the one with the small yellow flowers. Her umbrella would be open, the rain sliding off its red lacquered surface and pooling on the ground around her like a halo. In that moment, I wouldn't care that they had called her a fox. I wouldn't hesitate. I would run hard and fall into her arms. I would remember again what it felt like to be embraced by her.

Mama would wipe away my tears. She would tell me that it was okay, that I was going to be okay. And when she said it, it wouldn't have been a lie.

In my mind, my mother came back to me a million times. I've moved on, yes. I was living my life the best that I could. But seeing her now, before me, I realized that I had never stopped hoping, never stopped wishing, no matter how impossible it may have seemed.

"Hello, Nami." The woman closed her umbrella and smiled. She was so close. If I really wanted to, I could reach out and touch her. In my heart, I had already run to her. I had closed the gap between us and fallen into her arms. But when I looked down, I hadn't moved at all.

The warm starlight reflecting off the snow made the woman's skin luminous, almost otherworldly. I couldn't take my eyes off of her. She was beautiful, standing there alone, the snow silently falling all around her. Her thick black hair was swept away from her face, and a hair ornament with a tiny bell was placed in its folds. I could see her eyes now, those deep brown eyes, gazing straight through to my soul. Her eyes, that small nose, those perfect heart lips, I didn't want to believe that they were mine. But the longer I looked at her, the more I couldn't deny the resemblance. Before long, I could see with my own eyes what my father had seen years ago.

I don't know what I expected, but time had passed, hadn't it? The years apart from my father and I should have taken their toll. They should have weighed heavily on her. Even now, my own sadness should have been recognizable in my mother's face. But seeing her standing there was like seeing a lost child in my memory. No matter how many years had passed, this woman in front of me was still young and vibrant, as if misfortune had never once laid its hands on her.

"Nami," the woman said again. Suddenly, she stepped forward and embraced me. As those delicate arms wrapped around my shoulders, I almost jumped back. A part of me was surprised that she was real, that there was something to hold onto. I wanted to hug her with all my might. I wanted to cry the tears that I had held in for so long. But I just stood there, my arms firmly at my sides.

The man already knew. He could see it in my face. I couldn't just run to her. I couldn't just let her fill my heart. It wasn't that easy to let go of the past. It wasn't that easy to be reborn. No, in my eyes, he saw the questions running through my head, the confusion, the anger, and the many hardships. He knew that this meeting was just the beginning.

The woman pulled away from me finally. "I thought I would never see this day," she cried, wiping the tears from her eyes. "I missed you so much. To see you again, Nami, it's like a dream."

She was so young and full of life, as if every one of her dreams had come true. But something had changed within me. And now, I couldn't forgive that brightness. She didn't have a right to be happy. She didn't have a right to dream when all the while I'd been living this nightmare. That light around her made me feel like she wasn't sorry at all.

"Then why did you leave us?" My voice felt too loud in that delicate snowfield, but I couldn't help myself. I needed to know. I needed her to tell me. But she averted her gaze.

The anger began to build inside of me. In no time, it had choked every good feeling in my heart. That girlish look she gave me, made me feel like we had switched roles, like she had expected me to be the mother. And what I really needed so badly right now was to remember what it felt like to be her daughter.

"Is it true?" I pressed her.

"What do you mean?"

"Did you run off with another man?" The woman wouldn't meet my eyes. I knew it. My father was right, wasn't he? She *was* a fox. And if my mother was a fox, then I was definitely a fox daughter.

The woman shook her head. "It's not true at all."

"Then why did you leave us? Why did you leave me?"

"Nami." In that moment, I could see the pain suddenly bloom in my mother's face. But I couldn't stop myself.

"I saw you disappear. I saw it happen with my own eyes. And then I heard it. Even if I couldn't see you, I heard you walking away from me."

I was sobbing now, the sadness filling my whole being. In an instant, I was at that bridge. I was five again, and that nightmare was just beginning. "And when I told him, Papa didn't believe me. Do you know what it's like to have your own father not believe you? Eventually, you start doubting yourself."

"Nami." I covered my ears then. I didn't want her to explain. Everything that came out of her mouth now would just be an excuse. But my mother reached up and gently pulled my hands away from my ears. She searched my eyes for any glimmer of compassion, but I didn't feel generous at all.

"It's not what you think," the woman pleaded. "You have to believe me."

"How am I supposed to believe you? You left us. You ruined my father, and then he ruined me." The woman moved to embrace me again, but I shook her off. I didn't want her to think that a hug could make everything okay. It wasn't okay. It would never be okay. "I'm lucky Naoki and

Bachan saved me. Who else would have taken in a fox daughter?"

"You're not a fox daughter."

"How can you be so naïve? Everyone thought that you were a fox, even Papa!" There was pain in my mother's face. I couldn't deny that a part of me felt glad to have hit a nerve, to watch that brightness fade, even just a little.

"Your Papa was very very sad."

"So, it's okay then? I should've just let him touch me like I'm you?" That anger was so big inside of me now that I thought I was going to burst. All at once, the man pulled me into his arms and held me tight. In his embrace, I felt safe, like nothing or no one could hurt me. But I couldn't stop crying. Deep down, a part of me felt guilty. My own mother was standing not three feet away, but I didn't go to her. It should have been my mother comforting me. It should have been my mother holding me tight. But I didn't trust her.

"Nami," the man said. He whispered my name again and again until my heart had wrung out every last tear. Then he held my face in his hands and made me look at him. "What you saw that day was true."

"No, it wasn't. My father said it wasn't." He turned me around to face the woman again, but I didn't want to look at her.

"Tell her, Sanae."

"What do you mean?" I asked her.

The woman's face fell. No matter how hard my mother tried, she couldn't hide what she was feeling inside. The tears on her cheeks shone in the soft starlight as she and the man exchanged looks.

"I did disappear in front of you," she said finally.

"What?"

"That day, what you saw was true. I did disappear."

"I don't understand. Didn't you want to stay here? Didn't you want to stay with me? If you had, none of this would have ever happened."

"I very much wanted to stay with you and your father. You have to believe me, Nami. I didn't want to leave you."

"Then why?" The woman came closer. She touched my arm and looked deep into my eyes.

"Because by the time I arrived in Kasumi-machi again, I was already dead."

I searched her eyes. *This was a joke, right? Dead? How could she have been dead?* I turned back to the man, wanting him to tell me that she was lying. But his gaze was true.

"I don't believe you," I told her, desperately trying to make sense of her words.

"Nami."

"You died?"

"Yes."

"How can that be? If that's true, then how am I here?" I searched her face for answers, but my mother turned away from me. It was as if she didn't want to hear the questions in my head. She didn't want to see my pain.

"Sanae." My mother looked up at the man. He was staring hard at her as if willing her to speak. "She deserves to know the truth."

"But I don't want to hurt her anymore."

"You'll hurt her even more if you don't tell her." My mother knew the man was right, but she didn't answer right away. She wouldn't even look at me.

"Mama?"

Slowly, she turned around and met my gaze. "It was the night of the matsuri. In Kasumi-machi, everyone had gathered to pray for a good harvest. They were going to celebrate with lanterns and colorful floats, dancing and music. Everyone was going to be there, including the man I was about to marry."

"Papa?"

She shook her head. "I was only seventeen. I had never been in love before, but I knew that I could never find it with that man. And I didn't want him to take that one chance away from me. But I couldn't convince my mother."

"I don't understand."

"Do you remember the pine forest?"

"I do."

She smiled weakly through her tears. "That's where my father died. When they found his body, he was surrounded by a family of white foxes. My mother wouldn't let me see him. She said she didn't want me to remember him that way. But that was a lie."

"What do you mean?"

"My mother didn't trust the foxes. She thought they had lured my father across the bridge and into the forest. She blamed them for his death, even though it was obvious that he had fallen from a tree."

"Did you believe her?"

"In the beginning I did. She was the only person I had left, the only one I could hold onto. But my mother became a different person after my father died. She was so fearful. She clung to me until I couldn't breathe. I did whatever she asked. I promised I wouldn't go to the bridge. I promised I wouldn't look for the foxes. But when she told me that I would have to marry that man, that it was the only way to stay there in that house, a part of me would never forgive her."

I watched her face change in the glowing amber light. Years had passed, but my mother still couldn't let go of it. It wasn't just that she was holding on. I could see that anger in her face. It was old anger, the kind that had been there since the beginning of time. "Do you remember when we went to see the fox shrine?"

"The one in the pine tree?"

"Yes. My father made that shrine. He dedicated it to Inari after the foxes saved his life in a snowstorm. Only he and I knew about it. I didn't get to say goodbye to my father when he died. Maybe that's why a part of me believed that he was still alive, that he lived on inside of me. That's why I wanted you to see it that day. I knew that time was running out, and I wanted to give you something to hold onto."

"But a memory isn't enough, Mama."

"I know."

"Tell me what happened at the matsuri."

"When I couldn't convince my mother to change her mind, I vowed that I would become just like my father. Like him, I would stop being afraid."

My mother closed her eyes. In her heart, I knew that she was listening to the river rushing below the bridge. I knew this because I was her daughter, and for as long as I lived, I would never get tired of that sound.

"You were at the bridge."

"Yes. I was going to see my true love." She laughed to herself. "Even now, it sounds so naïve to say it out loud. My true love. It seemed like too much to ask."

"I don't think so." She smiled.

"They say you can see him in the pine forest. I wanted to know if it were true. At that point, I needed something to hold onto, something to make me believe that I wasn't beyond love. If I could just see the face of my true love, then I could go on living."

"Even if you had to marry another man?"

"Yes. I was resigned to my fate, but my best friend convinced me to go there that night. Besides my father, she was the only other person who understood my heart."

"Did you get to see him? Did you get to see your true love?"

She shook her head. "When I stepped onto the bridge, it began to wobble with my weight. Soon, I could barely stand upright without being in danger of falling over. Takako called me back, but I couldn't give up. This was my only chance."

"What happened?"

"The bridge collapsed. I didn't even get a chance to tell Takako goodbye."

"But then, how—"

"The gods took pity on me. I was so young when it happened. I hadn't really lived a life yet, so I was given a second chance."

"Like being reborn?"

"In a way. I was allowed to come back and soothe my mother's heart, to say goodbye. But I was too late."

"Too late?"

"I waited too long. Even death couldn't take away that resentment I felt toward my mother. At the time, I blamed her for everything. When I finally decided to make the trip back, many many years had already passed in the earthly world, and I was returning to a Kasumi-machi where my mother was no longer living. Now, there was no reason to stay, no one's heart to soothe, no one to say goodbye to."

"But didn't you want to see her?" My mother's look grew far away.

"I did," she said to me finally. "But I wasn't as brave as you, Nami."

"But you came back."

"I know. But by then, I had already met your father. And meeting him changed everything."

- 20 -

MY MOTHER TURNED TO LOOK AT ME, but her gaze was still somewhere else. She didn't need to tell me. I knew that in her mind, she had already left the field of snow, the Eternal Night. She was running through the pine forest and across the bridge. And on the other side, in the Kasumi-machi of her memory, he was already waiting for her.

All of a sudden, she didn't look like my mother at all. What I was seeing before me was a girl like me. My mother was seventeen again. She had fallen in love for the first time. She had dreams and desires. She made mistakes. She had her hopes dashed. She thought that she would die without him. She loved him with all her heart.

In that moment, I probably understood my mother more than she would ever know. Even in the darkness of the Eternal Night, or the glow of this snowfield, I could still hear his voice, "Even just once would be enough." Naoki and I were separated by time and space, but our hearts were always connected. I could feel it.

When my mother finally met my gaze, her eyes were filled with light, as if she were returning from a dream.

"Do you know the legend of Kasumi?"

I shook my head. "If you told me, I don't remember. It was so long ago." My mother smiled, but she couldn't hide her disappointment.

"Well, it doesn't matter now," she laughed. "It was just a silly story anyway."

"Did she really exist?"

My mother's face lit up again. "Yes, Nami. It was such a long long time ago, but Kasumi really did exist. She was the only daughter of a court lady and very very beautiful. She had many suitors, but like me, she was forced to marry a man she didn't love. I imagine the ache in her heart was far greater than mine. By that time, she had already found her true love.

"What happened to them?"

"Her lover died on that bridge, trying to save her."

"He died?" My mother nodded.

"Kasumi couldn't bear her grief and lived the rest of her years alone in the pine forest. My father told me that on summer nights, after the rains, when the mist is in the air, go to the bridge and stand in the middle of it. If your heart is pure, the mist will clear for a moment, and in the darkened forest, Kasumi will show you the face of your true love."

"Did you believe it?"

"At first, I didn't. How could I? There was no reason to see the face of my true love now, not when my mother had already promised me to another. Luckily, Takako didn't agree with me."

"That's why you were at the bridge."

"Yes."

"But you found your true love in the end."

My mother turned away from me then. It was as if she didn't want me to see her face. She didn't want me to see how much she still loved my father.

"I did," she said finally. "But I was lucky."

"I don't understand."

"After I realized that my mother was no longer here, I was going to return. But then, I met your father. He was so kind. I thought to myself, maybe I could just stay here for a day. What would it matter to linger?"

"But you fell in love."

She nodded. "There wasn't a day that went by when I didn't return to the bridge. Each morning, I vowed to myself that I would finally do it. I would steady my heart and return to the snowfield where I belonged. But the longer I stayed, the more time I wanted. Eventually, I stopped going to the bridge. There was no need. I was in love."

"Then why did you leave us, Mama? Why did you leave Papa and me?"

"I had no choice. That day, when we went to the fox shrine, I knew something was about to happen. I had seen the Akita near the house. He had come to take me back. I was sure of it."

"Why did you take me then?"

"Because you had suffered too long because of me. I couldn't deny you such a beautiful day. And I wanted you to see that fox shrine for yourself."

"Is that why you always prayed for long life?"

"Of course. I didn't want to leave. I thought if I made an offering to Inari, she would take pity on me, and I would be safe, or at least, she would give me more time. But you were just like me. You fell in love with the sound of water. Deep in your heart, you loved nothing more than being suspended over a rushing river. Was it not like flying?"

It was. That day, the sound of water filled my body. It rooted itself in my heart so much so that I couldn't escape it. Above that river, I felt alive, like I was seeing everything for the first time.

"But when I saw you there on the bridge," my mother began, "I did what only a mother would. I thought only about my child."

Tears were flowing down her cheeks now. She grabbed my shoulders and held me firmly in her hands. "I didn't want to leave you and your Papa!" She sobbed. "You must believe me, Nami. If I could, I would have stayed there with you forever. But as a mother, I wasn't thinking about myself. I only wanted to save you."

Mama fell to the ground, clutching at her chest. Her voice felt loud across the snowfield. But I couldn't comfort her. All I could do was stand there and watch. A part of me felt so ashamed. This whole time, I had only thought about my own pain. I hadn't realized what my mother had endured. I had only thought about what she had left behind.

I sat down beside her. "Where did you go, Mama?" My mother looked up at me then. Her face was red and stained with tears, but I could still make out my face in her own.

"Because I stepped onto the bridge, I had no choice but to return to the Weeping Field. The bridge was where I died in my first life. When you return to the place you died, you will definitely go back."

The man cleared his throat. My mother had spun such a wonderful tale that I had almost forgotten that he was there. "Is that the name of this place? The Weeping Field?"

He nodded. I gazed out across the snowfield to the pine trees that stood guard. They seemed so much larger and older here than even the ones in the pine forest.

"Does the sun ever rise here?" I asked the man.

"No. Even in the Weeping Field, the night is endless."

I couldn't imagine what it was like to live where it was always night. I didn't care how beautiful the stars were. Being here in the darkness, I longed so much to see the blue sky again. I wondered if my mother longed to see it too.

"I should have gone back that first day," my mother said to me. She stood up again, her yukata covered in snow. "But I was young, and I hadn't experienced love in my short life. I believe now that Inari had taken pity on me. In those five years that I spent with you and your father, she allowed me to live. This is why in the end, I was able to accept her judgment.

"Judgment?"

"Your mother broke the rules," the man said.

"What harm could there be in falling in love?"

"That's not how things work here. You are given the chance to say goodbye to someone, not live another life."

"What will happen to my mother now?"

"She will have to atone for her actions. She will have to stay here in the Weeping Field."

My eyes fell on the stars glowing in the snow. I could see why it was called the Weeping Field. All those tears froze and hardened. To be reborn here, was like having one's grief suspended in time. Each day, the stars fell to the ground. Each day, there was another chance to go back, to move on. But it wasn't easy to see this as a gift. I wondered how long my mother would have to stay in a place like this. Would she ever leave?

The man shook his head as if he could read my mind. "No, the Weeping Field is not eternal," he said. "You cannot stay here forever. It's a place to wait, a place to decide."

"Who gets to be reborn here?"

"Usually, people who didn't get the chance to say goodbye."

"Like the people in the tsunami?"

He nodded. "And children too."

"But not Papa."

"No."

"Why not? Was it because he wasn't nice to the foxes?" I glanced at my mother. She wasn't listening. Her gaze was still focused far across that snowfield.

The man looked at me hard. "No, it's not that simple. Deep in his heart, your father had already said goodbye."

I thought about my father then. He must have been cold, lying there alone in that hospital. To the very end, he couldn't let go. He couldn't go on living without my mother. A love that strong should have carried him straight to her after he died. I was surprised that he wasn't reborn here. To me, he seemed like someone who needed to apologize, someone who needed to say goodbye.

- 21 -

WE STOOD THERE, THE THREE OF US, NOT SAYING A WORD. I was sure my mother was still thinking about my father. Her gaze was fixed beyond the snowfield, as if she could somehow reclaim that life. Maybe she wanted to know where Papa was. Deep down, maybe she had hoped that he, too, would have been reborn here. I looked at her face. No matter how much she loved me, it was clear that her heart was still with him. I tried to understand her, but I couldn't forget the darkness I was carrying.

"Did you know?" I asked her. The moment I said it, my mother's face filled with pain. She knew what I was talking about. I could see it.

"I don't understand," she replied. Deep in her heart, I knew she was ashamed. She couldn't even look at me then.

172

"Did you know what Papa did?"

She didn't want to answer me, but the truth was too big to ignore. "I didn't. But even if I did, I can't believe it. I can't believe that he would do such a thing. That wasn't the man I loved. Isao would never have hurt you. He loved you so much. You were literally the center of his world."

At the sound of her words, I could feel that anger burn up inside of me. I wanted to scream, yell, cry, anything to keep from exploding. *How could she say that! How could she take his side? Didn't she care what happened to me?* Just as I was about to burst, I felt the man's hands rest on my shoulders.

"Nami." He said my name again, but I didn't want to answer him. I didn't want him to talk me out of my feelings. But he turned me around until I was facing those soft brown eyes. "Think hard about what you want to say to her. Hurting her will not change what happened to you."

"But—"

"Even if your mother did know, she wouldn't have been able to help you. No matter how much it hurt her, she had to stay here, in the Weeping Field."

"But I was her child," I cried. "Doesn't that matter? Doesn't that mean anything?" Tears filled my eyes, and the man became a blur.

"Nothing has changed. You're still her child. You will always be her child, Nami. Yes, you deserved a better life.

You deserved a father who loved you and cared about you, not a monster. But hating her, won't bring those years back."

Deep down, I knew he was right. Even if I didn't want to admit it, the man had spoken the truth. But I couldn't let him in. I dried my eyes and turned to face my mother again. She wouldn't look at me. Even now, she couldn't reconcile the man she loved with the one who had hurt me. There was a part of her that didn't want to. I could see it.

"You still love him," I said.

"How can I not? He gave me you! And to have had a daughter, even if it was just for five years, was such a precious gift. In a way, I felt like I had redeemed myself in my mother's eyes."

"You got to enjoy the good part, Mama. You didn't have to face the consequences of your actions."

"Do you wish that you had never been born?" Her eyes were pleading in that moment. She knew the answer, but she was still hoping that I would tell her different.

"Yes, I wish I had never been born. At night, when he'd come to my room—"

She covered her ears. "I don't want to hear it!"

"No, Mama. I want you to hear it. I don't want to be carrying this burden by myself for the rest of my life. If you hadn't left us, none of this would have ever happened."

In that moment, I didn't realize how much I hated her for leaving, how much I had been holding onto, how much grief had been shoved down, untouched. The man took me into his arms again. I held onto him tight as if my life depended on it.

"Nami, is this what you really want? Can you honestly say that you didn't want to be born?"

"Yes," I said into his chest.

"But it was because you were born, because your father did what he did to you, that you were at the river that day."

I pulled away from him. "How did you know?"

"I'm a guardian of the underworld. It's my job to know people's stories." He smiled at me. "And because you were at the river, didn't you meet someone?"

"I did." In that moment, I saw Naoki standing behind me, telling me not to do it, not to jump in.

"Wasn't it just like fate?"

"It was," I admitted.

"And didn't you fall in love?"

"Yes. But it doesn't matter now, does it? He's dead. He's been gone for three months."

"Do you still love him?" I began crying, and he held me to him tight.

"Yes."

"Do you still miss him?"

"Yes."

"Will that change even after you tell your mother everything you want to say?"

I shook my head. Even after I told her everything, it still wouldn't bring Naoki back. It still wouldn't bring my mother back and the life that we had. I pulled away from the man's embrace and looked back at my mother.

In that amber glow, I saw my own pain reflected in her face for the first time. They say a fox woman is too beautiful to resist. Men are weak creatures. There are some that go crazy when she disappears. But no one ever talks about the fox. Even a dead woman was allowed to feel love, to feel longing.

"What is his name?" My mother asked me after a while.

"Who?"

"The one who lives on in your heart."

"Naoki. His name is Naoki." My mother said his name quietly to herself, as if she were trying to imagine what he looked like.

"Did you love him?"

"Yes, with all my heart. I still do. We have a child, a daughter named Suzu." In that moment, my mother's eyes lit up. They were so clear and bright and filled with joy. I didn't have to say anything more. Her tears said it all.

"Is that why you came? For your child?"

I nodded. "But I didn't know that this would be my destination. I was only trying to find my daughter."

"What do you mean?"

"Suzu and I were on our way home from the fox shrine when she saw something on the bridge. You remember the Akita?"

"Yes, I do. But what does he have to do with her?"

"When she saw the Akita, she just took off after him. I couldn't stop her. No matter how many times I called to her, she wouldn't listen. Before I knew it, she had disappeared into the pine forest. And that's the last I saw of her."

"Oh, Nami."

"I don't know where she is now. I don't know how to find her. I just did what a mother would do. Did I make a mistake?"

"No. You did the right thing. You thought only of your child." In that moment, I realized that my mother and I were the same. We had both forsaken our own happiness for the sake of our daughters. A part of me felt closer to her then. All this time, my mother had to live with her decision. She wasn't immune to the consequences at all. She, too, had been carrying around the darkness. She, too, had tried to put the sunshine before her.

"I tried to take you with me that day," she said all of a sudden.

"What?"

"I tried to take you with me. But you couldn't see me. I was there as you cried, as you called out to me."

"You saw me? You were still there?"

"Of course. I didn't care that the Akita was waiting for me, that he was going to take me back. I couldn't leave you. But I was already dead. There was no way for a ghost to lead a human into the next world—at least not on my own."

I looked into my mother's eyes. She was crying now. I could feel her pain much more than she knew. "I never knew that, Mama."

"You couldn't have. But it's true. You have to believe me, Nami. I didn't want to leave you."

- 22 -

SOMETHING HAD SHIFTED. I could feel it. All that anger I had
been holding onto so tightly had suddenly burned away. I
felt free. My heart was growing with love. I couldn't explain
it, but it was like Mama and I had finally turned a page.

We stood there for a long time not saying a word. It was
as if we were letting the love flow between us once again.

All of a sudden, my mother took my hands in hers.
"Why not stay here with me?" she said. Her eyes were
bright and shining. "To have found you again is like a gift
from the gods, one I thought I would never be given."

"She's human, Sanae," the man interjected.

"What does it matter? Isn't this like fate that I should
meet her again after all this time?"

"She doesn't belong here."

"But she is half of me! Half of her was born of a dead woman," my mother cried.

"Still, there are rules we must follow."

"It doesn't matter," my mother began. "Once Inari finds out that she's here, will she really let her go back after all she has seen?"

"That's for Inari to decide."

"And what about my grandchild? How will you find her?"

The man stared hard at my mother. He wasn't going to make any exceptions. "That's not your problem. Don't worry. I will find her. And then, I will return your daughter and granddaughter to their own world."

I touched my mother's hands. They were warm and soft. Even my young hands couldn't compare with her beauty. Down the line and through the years, my hands will grow old and wrinkled, while my mother's will always remain smooth. She will never have to hide them in her lap or under a kimono sleeve like Bachan sometimes does. My mother will never have to feel that way. She will always be young.

"Mama! Mama!" Even in the depths of the Weeping Field, I could hear my daughter's voice, calling to me. She was alive in here, somewhere. She had to be. *Wait for me, Suzu. I'm coming.*

Mama smiled. "What is it, Nami?"

"Thank you."

"What for?"

"All this time, the memory of you was buried in my heart. I thought I couldn't truly love anyone else. But seeing you now, I realized that my heart has gotten bigger. It can love so much deeper than it did before."

"That's why you must stay here, Nami. We have so much time to make up for. You don't have to leave. I know the gods will take pity on me, as you are my child."

"No, Mama. I want to go back. I need to go back."

"Why?"

"Because my daughter is there and Bachan is there. I know deep in my heart that they're waiting for me to return."

In that moment, this life, this human life became so precious to me. It began to mean everything. The Weeping Field was truly beautiful, but it would never change. Time stopped here. If these people could accept it with their whole hearts, Inari's gift was so much greater than they could ever realize. She was giving people the chance to move forward. All they had to do was take it. But even the dead were afraid. It took all of them to believe that joy was waiting just on the other side.

"But we will not be together, Nami."

"We will. My heart is big enough now. I can love many many people. There's room for you *and* my daughter."

She began to cry. I was about to apologize, but she waved me away and turned back to the forest at the edge of the snowfield. "Is it not amazing that even in this snow, the pine trees still flourish?"

"This place is magical, isn't it?"

Mama turned to look at me again. "But even in your world, they stay ever green, even in winter when everything else has fallen into a deep deep sleep."

"That's true."

"Only the pines are awake then and the lonely foxes. But you've learned how to be a pine tree, how to stay ever green in your own world."

I smiled. "And are you going to be a lonely fox?"

"No, my time in the Weeping Field will not be forever. One day, I'm sure that I will move on to the next world."

"I'm glad."

"Are you sure, Nami? Are you sure you don't want to stay here?"

"You're my mother and seeing you again was the best thing that has ever happened to me. But I need to go back. I don't want my daughter to be alone. I don't want her to suffer any more than she already has."

My mother didn't look at me then. In that moment, she appeared almost like a child. In fact, I felt older than her, as if I really were her mother. "I was selfish to fall in love, wasn't I?" she said.

"A part of me wants to tell you that you should have come back just to say goodbye. You asked for too much to fall in love. And then, when you left, Papa just couldn't recover. His heart was always searching for you. But another part of me is so proud that you were brave enough to fall in love. If you hadn't made that choice, I wouldn't be here. I wouldn't have met Naoki. I wouldn't have had my daughter. And I wouldn't have met a guardian of the underworld." I looked back at the man and smiled. His eyes were gleaming.

"What can I do?" she asked. "What can I do to make you stay?"

"You can't do anything." Mama was weeping now, her voice getting lost in the snow.

"But I couldn't do anything for you. I couldn't protect you at all. And now, you're alone."

"I'm not alone. I have my daughter and Bachan. And I have you. Mama, you have been there all along, in every single person that I have ever met who has been kind to me. Your heart was in Naoki. And my child will know your heart too. I'll make sure of it."

Mama smiled at me. "Nami."

"Mama, I will live my life to the fullest, for the both of us. I will love for the both of us. I will cry. I will get angry. I will feel joy for the both of us. So, don't worry about me. You can move on now. Papa, wherever he is, has been waiting for you for such a long, long time."

My mother was crying again. Even as she wept, she was beautiful. In that moment, I heard a steady ticking in the quiet of the snowfield. I looked down. It was Naoki's watch. Since the accident, it had stopped working, but now, I could feel its heart beating again as if it had somehow come back to life. I gazed at the face and felt a rush of love in my heart. I touched it one last time as if it were really Naoki's face. Then I handed it to my mother. She hesitated to take it, but I took her hand, placed the watch inside and closed her fingers around it.

My mother looked at the watch. She touched the face as if she were seeing her true love in its reflection.

"Is it okay?" Mama asked. I nodded.

"If you see Naoki, please give it to him."

"Don't you want to hold onto it?" I did. A million times over, I did. But a watch wasn't going to bring him back. And holding onto it wasn't going to help me move forward.

I shook my head. "Let time start again, Mama."

She smiled. I reached out and put my arms around her then. She was as tiny as I was. It almost felt like I was hugging myself. "This is how a mother's embrace feels," I told her finally.

"Nami," she said. "You're going to be such a great mother."

- 23 -

As the man and I rode back into the night, I could see Mama through the pines. She was standing in the middle of the snowfield, waving goodbye. The light from the stars still touched my face, but my mother grew smaller and smaller in my vision, until she faded like a dream.

"Mama!" I cried. "Mama!" But it was too late. In that moment, the weight of my choice sat heavy in my heart. I wanted to jump off that horse. I wanted to run back to the Weeping Field and tell my mother that I had made a mistake, that I wanted to stay with her. But the man held me to him tight, as if he knew my heart. He wasn't going to let me go, no matter how deep my grief. After a while, I was too tired to fight him anymore. I closed my eyes, and before long, I had fallen asleep in his arms.

By the time I opened my eyes again, the darkness was beginning to fade. Soon, the sky grew light, and pale streaks of orange and pink reached across the heavens. My heart swelled with relief. I couldn't believe it. After all this time in the night, the dawn had finally come.

"Look," the man whispered. "It's morning." My eyes flooded with tears. Until that moment, I hadn't realized how much I had missed the dawn. Even as we began to ascend the mountain, I never took my eyes off the sky. The higher we went, the brighter it grew. When the sun finally broke through the clouds, I knew we weren't going back. We had left the Eternal Night for good. Wherever we were headed now, spring was beginning again.

All morning, the man's horse climbed at a steady gait. We were ascending, higher and higher into the light, but even in that brightness, I couldn't ignore the sting of loss in my chest. I kept looking down the mountain, searching for her through the pines. But no matter how many times I looked back, all I saw was just an endless sea of trees. Mama, the stars, and even the snowfield had disappeared forever. Now, I didn't know what to believe.

"Don't worry," the man said. "She's there." Yes, Mama was there, but there was so far away. Without her here, I wondered if the mother I had seen before me was real or just a figment of my imagination. After all this time, we were finally together. *Why didn't I choose to stay with her? She's my mother. I should've chosen her.* I sighed and rested my head against the man's chest. "You made the right decision," he said. "It may not feel like it now, but in time, you'll see."

Deep down, I knew he was right, but it just didn't feel that way. All that talk back there about wanting to go back to Kasumi-machi, wanting to live the joys and sorrows of human life felt so different after leaving her. It wasn't fair. *How could anyone choose between their mother and their child?* And even now, I wasn't sure that I had made the right choice.

"Why did you let me see her?" I asked him. "You said you were going to take me back. You said there were rules you couldn't break."

I looked up at him then. I wanted to see his eyes when he answered me. I wanted to know that what he said was true. But when I met his gaze, his tenderness broke straight through to my heart. The man smiled to himself. In that moment, it was as if he were remembering something from long, long ago.

"Because I was protecting your heart," he said to me finally.

"My heart?"

"Your mother was where everything began. If you didn't get to see her again, you would never be able to move on. You would never be able to truly love your daughter. You would always be wondering. And your heart would always be saving that space for your mother."

"But why would you do that for me? You hardly know me."

The man's eyes were bright, shining with joy, "But I do. Probably more than you know."

"I don't understand."

"Because I vowed to protect you for all eternity."

I stared at him for a long time, not quite understanding his words. Then, all at once, the immensity of what he had just said filled my entire being.

"You mean?"

"That's right." *There must be some mistake.* No one gave their life for me. No one protected me except for Naoki and Bachan. And even so, things like this didn't happen in real life, did they? "It's not a dream, Nami."

Suddenly, I found myself weeping. But I wasn't sad. These were new tears. They were tears of joy and happiness. They were tears of love. The man's face beamed. Now I knew. I was Kasumi. I was the girl who was his family, the one he had given his life for, the one he vowed to protect in that life and every life thereafter.

"Then you were the one I loved?"

"Yes."

"And you were the one who fell from the bridge?"

"I was only trying to save your life." The man turned his gaze to the sky above us, but I could see tears pooling in his eyes. In my heart, I felt something quiver. He had touched a part of me that I thought had died when Naoki passed away. After all this time, I hadn't realized just how much I was loved.

"Why would you do that for me?"

"It's simple. Because I loved you."

"Me?" The man nodded.

"I wanted to protect you from your father in this life, but I was too late." He was weeping now. I touched his cheek, and his tears fell onto my skin. "I couldn't keep you safe. That alone tore me apart."

"But it wasn't your fault," I said to him.

"But what you had to endure, what you had to give up, it was unforgivable."

"There's nothing to forgive."

"I wish I could have done more for you." I shook my head. The man looked so sad then. I wanted to take his face in my hands and wipe away his tears. I wanted to whisper to him again and again that he was the one who had given me my life back.

"You've done enough," I told him. He pulled me close again. It was so strange. I had just met him, but now, it felt like I had known him my whole life.

"You may not know it," the man began again, "but I have been there with you all along, Nami. I have been there protecting your heart."

"I don't understand."

"I protected your heart so that you could love, so that whatever happened in your life, whatever hardship you faced, you wouldn't shut out the world. And even if it was just for eight years, I was so lucky."

"Eight years?" It couldn't be. I pulled away from him and looked into his eyes, but he wouldn't meet my gaze.

"But now, Nami, it's time for you to move forward." All at once, I knew that voice. Why hadn't I recognized it sooner? I had heard it a million times before, a million more in my heart. I burst into tears. *Had I forgotten it already? Had I forgotten him?*

"Wait! What do you mean? Tell me what you mean." I was sobbing now. "Naoki."

The man pulled me into his arms. "In every lifetime, I have looked for you," he whispered. "I have protected your heart. That was my vow." I closed my eyes. That voice that I had only heard in my dreams was here, real, before me.

My heart hurt so badly. All those days of longing and grief rushed to the surface, and I was helpless to stop it.

"Why did you leave me?" I wailed.

"It was my time, Nami. Maybe in the next life, we'll get it right. We'll grow old together."

"No, I don't want to wait until the next life. I don't want to go on without you."

"Nami." He touched my face. I didn't want him to tell me that I couldn't stay with him, that there were rules we had to follow. I didn't want to hear it. I just wanted him to hold me. I wanted to pretend that we still had a lifetime together.

He looked deep into my eyes. He didn't look anything like Naoki, but I would never forget the way he looked at me. Those eyes were his. They were the same eyes that stared at me that day at the river. In that moment, there were so many things I wanted to ask him, so much I wanted to say, but all I could do was bring my lips to his. He didn't hesitate. He was real. He covered my mouth with his and kissed me deeply, as if he had been starved this whole time in the darkness. I was breathless when he pulled away. I wanted more. I wanted to be with him forever, even if that meant that I would never get to see the dawn, that I would never get to see my daughter or Bachan again.

But when he looked into my eyes, I wished we could go back to when I didn't know yet that our forever wasn't written in the stars.

- 24 -

We were silent as we neared the top of that mountain. In the sky, the sun was rising, golden and bright, but by that time, I had hardly noticed. My head was spinning. I could still feel his lips on mine. I could feel the weight of his longing. In that moment, all I wanted to do was hold him. I wanted to stay there in his arms forever, instead of grasping at a memory.

He couldn't take me back now. I convinced myself that he wouldn't. We had crossed a threshold. We had found each other again across time and space. There was no way he was going to let me go.

Where we finally stopped, there was a small clearing. All around us, the pines were ancient, almost prehistoric, like they had seen the beginning of time. I didn't know where we were but somehow, I wasn't afraid. Here, on this mountain, I could breathe again. I could hear the birds calling out to each other. I could feel the wind caress my face. Because of Naoki, I could feel myself coming alive again after so long in the darkness.

"We need to walk from here." His voice seemed loud in that quiet, and he didn't look at me when he said it. Naoki's attention was already focused on the trail ahead. I didn't know how we would make it up that sharp ascent. There were jagged rocks everywhere. But he held out his hand and pulled me up to the next ledge and the next. Slowly, we moved on. All that time, he didn't say anything to me. He was silent, probably as lost in thought as I was.

No matter how hard the ascent, I found myself looking at him. Even now, it amazed me that Naoki's soul looked like this. He was charismatic. His presence filled the whole forest. In that moment, I wondered how such an expansive spirit had fit into Naoki's lanky body. I would never know for sure who this man was, but deep down, I didn't care. I trusted my heart. And all I knew was, he felt more real to me than even my own mother.

The air at the top of the mountain was crisp like an autumn day. I pulled my sweater tight, even as the sun traveled higher in the sky. Naoki didn't say a word. He stood there for a long time, listening to the wind. If I closed my eyes, I could still feel his kiss, his lips on mine, the way he tasted, and that voice I had heard a million times in my dreams. Even now, I felt it echoing in my body.

Behind us, a grove of bamboo trees descended down the mountain side. There were thousands of them, fit so close together, I couldn't see what lay ahead. I didn't care. Naoki would know the way. He had brought me this far, and I was grateful that I wouldn't have to face another forest alone. But when I turned back to look at him, he didn't make any attempt to move.

"Aren't we going down the mountain?" I asked him finally. He met my eyes. All of a sudden, I could feel the pain in his heart and the heaviness of his grief. "What's wrong?"

He reached out and took my hands in his. "Nami, this is as far as I can take you."

"What do you mean? I don't understand." He couldn't look at me then. "Naoki?"

"You, alone, must convince Inari to let you go back. I cannot go with you." He let go of my hands. I watched as he turned away from me then and headed back down the trail. I closed my eyes. *This must be a dream*, I told myself. *It was all just a bad dream. Wake up! Wake up, Nami!* But when I opened my eyes, he was getting farther and farther away from me.

"Wait!" I cried. Naoki stopped, but he wouldn't turn around. I ran to the edge of the clearing. I ran until I was right in front of him. I searched his eyes, for any understanding, but his gaze was already back in the Eternal Night. "Naoki, there's so much I want to say, so much I want to ask. And what about Suzu? You can't leave me until we find her!" But he wasn't listening to me.

"When you reach the other side of this bamboo grove, you will enter an orchard of peach trees. In the midst of those trees, there is a large lake. You will know it, because from a distance, the surface will appear shiny like glass. Rising from the water will be a tall red building like a Shinto shrine and surrounding it will be a field of white lotuses. When you see these things, you will know that you have reached Inari's domain. Tell her what is in your heart, and she will help you."

"Why are you doing this, Naoki? I've just found you again and now you're going to leave?"

"I cannot go with you. No matter how much I want to, no matter how much it hurts me." When he looked at me, his eyes were full of tears.

"But I love you. I don't want us to end this way. It's too painful! I lost you once. I'm not going to lose you again."

"You will never lose me, Nami."

"But you won't be here with me. Don't you care about finding Suzu? Don't you care about me? Do you know how hard it has been without you? Some days, I just don't have the courage to go on. I miss you so much, Naoki. I miss you so much it hurts."

He looked deep into my eyes. "I know. I miss you too, even more so now. But I cannot go with you."

"Why not?"

"Nami," he said. "I live in the land of darkness now. That is my place. I cannot cross over into the land of the living, and Inari's domain is there." Naoki's face was so human now. Those brown eyes were even softer and more tender, when they looked at me.

"But I don't want to do this without you. I need you," I pleaded.

"I cannot go. You must do this part on your own."

"I can't, Naoki." By that time, I was crying so hard that for a moment there, he became a blur. My heart felt like it was going to burst. I thought I had lost him. But then, his strong hands came to rest on my shoulders again.

"You will never be alone. There will always be people to help you, to love you, and when it is your turn to cross into the Eternal Night, I will be here, waiting for you, and together, you and I will walk again."

I looked up at him. His eyes were so kind, so gentle. In the daylight, he didn't look like a god of the underworld at all. The way he looked at me, I felt like he was true, that what he had promised was true.

"But you said that you would be here for me, that you would protect me for all eternity." He smiled a gentle smile. He reached for my hand and placed it on his heart.

"I am here, always."

"Naoki, please."

He touched my face one last time. "Even as you sleep, I'll be moving the stars for you." He lingered there for just a moment longer as if he were trying to imprint this moment in his heart, as if he were trying to keep my face in his memory forever. And then he walked away, back towards the Eternal Night.

I stood there and watched until I couldn't see him any longer. Deep down, I prayed that he would come running back, that he'd tell me that this was all a big mistake. I thought he would at least turn around and wave. But not once did he ever look back.

- 25 -

No matter the distance between us, my heart longed to be back in the Eternal Night. I could still feel Naoki's kiss and the way he held me in his arms. I could still feel his heart beat against mine. Deep down, I wanted to believe him. I wanted to believe that he was still here, that this wasn't the end. But I couldn't convince my heart.

I was lonely in this forest. All around me, the bamboo had grown so thick, I couldn't see the sky anymore. I couldn't even see where the trail ended. My only friend was the wind, whistling through the trees. Every now and then, I would hear something skitter behind me, and I'd pray it would be him. But when I turned around, no one was there. I couldn't even see the way back.

I kept telling myself that it wouldn't be long now, that at some point, this green tunnel down the mountain had to end. But in my heart, I felt lost. Without Naoki, I didn't know where I was going or what I was supposed to do.

"Tell her what is in your heart," he had said. But there was so much in my heart that I wouldn't know where to begin. I had never met a fox goddess before.

The forest path began to level off. A few steps more and I knew I'd be at the valley floor. From where I stood, the afternoon light reached inside, beckoning me forward. It was so soft and welcoming. If I could let go, if I could just walk into it, I knew that I'd be in Inari's domain. And just beyond that, across the bridge was Kasumi-machi and Suzu.

I should have been running toward that light. There should have been no hesitation. But the truth is, I didn't want to go back. Mama was here. My love was here. I couldn't just leave. I remembered what Naoki had said, but I didn't think that I could do it anymore. *How was I supposed to convince Inari all by myself?* And the thought of moving on without him, was almost unbearable.

Just as I was about to turn back, I felt something brush against my cheek. I looked up. Where the sun was beginning to stream in through the trees, it was snowing. The soft white flakes fell onto my hair, my clothes, even scattering onto the ground around me. But it wasn't snow. I held out my hand, and a single white petal came to rest there. Peach blossoms.

Something so beautiful must be a sign. I held the petal in my hand like an amulet and placed it over my heart. Naoki had to be here. He had to be following me all along. I turned to look back one more time. I wanted to see him. *Even just once would be enough.* But the bamboo had already closed in behind me. There was no way back. No matter how much I wished it were different, I had no choice but to go on without him.

"Goodbye, Naoki," I whispered to the wind. I hoped it would take my love to him, all the way to the Eternal Night, straight to his heart. I wiped away my tears and took in a deep breath. And then, I walked into the light.

In my wildest dreams, I couldn't have imagined a place more alive. Things were breathing here in the land of the living. They grew and ripened. As far as my eyes could see, the valley floor was covered with peach trees. I stood there in awe, the spring snow filling the air around me. I didn't care that the petals were getting caught in the folds of my clothes or tangled in my hair. I couldn't get enough of them. There was something so happy about peach blossoms. It was like each one held the laughter and promise of spring time. All at once, I found myself reaching up to the sky. I wanted to grab hold of that happiness for myself. I wanted to remember what it felt like to shine.

Standing in that orchard, I felt like a child again. I was smiling. My hands were full of peach blossoms, and my heart was beating with a familiar joy. In that moment, I spotted the lake in the distance. It was just as Naoki had said. The surface of the water looked like glass. As I got closer, the gray blue lake transformed into a turquoise sea, and from its depths, a field of white lotuses reached for the sun. In the center, a tall red pagoda rose from the water. Adorned with a golden roof, the shoji doors on every floor were left open to the breeze.

I don't know what I was expecting, but Inari's home took me by surprise. Deep down, maybe I thought she would live somewhere more natural and unpainted, a thatched roof, maybe a hearth in the center of the house to cook and keep the place warm. But the fox goddess's house wasn't like that at all. It looked more like a Shangri-la, regal and bright, as if she ruled a whole kingdom.

The sky began to rain blossoms again, and the scent of peaches permeated the air. I felt like I was getting closer, like I was really returning home. Moments later, I could see Bachan waving to me from beyond the forest. She was standing at the edge of the bridge, holding a little girl's hand.

"Mama!" she cried. Suzu ran toward me as fast as she could. I ran from the forest, across the bridge, and lifted her into my arms. For the first time in a long time, she laughed with joy and squeezed me tight. It was as if we hadn't seen each other for such a long, long time. In that moment, I realized just how much I missed her, how much I didn't want to lose her.

Suzu touched my face as if she wanted to make sure that I was real. I smiled at her. I couldn't believe that she was really here.

When I opened my eyes again, the moon was in the sky. I wasn't standing at the edge of the lake anymore. Instead, I found myself lying on the pagoda's veranda, covered with a soft wool blanket. Across the floor, a woman with long white hair waited at a low table. She was stunning with deep-set eyes and full red lips. The kimono she wore was loose fitting, and aside from the blood red obi, it gleamed with the spring snow of a thousand peach blossoms.

"Please," she said as she gestured toward the tea and wagashi in front of her. Her voice was so gentle, I couldn't refuse. I found myself sitting up and lifting the blue cup to my nose. Peaches. And when I took a sip, my whole body became warm and calm. There was something very familiar about this scene. Even the way the warmth traveled down to my heart; I knew I had felt it before.

Against the black lacquered table, the wagashi almost glowed. It was shaped into a lonely summer peach garnished with yellow chrysanthemum petals. I bit into it. The taste was so nostalgic, I wanted to cry. There was something so natural about being here. I couldn't explain it. I was enjoying my wagashi and tea as if I were sitting across from an old friend, even though I didn't know her at all.

But the whole time I was enjoying her hospitality, the woman sat there in silence. She didn't join me with tea and sweets of her own. Instead, she took her time, studying me intently with those deep-set eyes.

"Nami, is it?" she asked all of a sudden.

"Yes, how did you know my name?"

"It doesn't matter. What does matter is why you are here. What brings you to the land of the living?" No matter how natural it had felt to be with her earlier, I could feel my confidence slipping away. I wasn't ready to make my case. I didn't know what to say to her to make her understand. *Tell her what is in your heart*, Naoki had said.

"I am here to see Inari," I began. "You see, I've been to the Weeping Field. I have seen my mother. I know that I'm not supposed to be here. But I wasn't trying to enter the underworld at all. I didn't mean any harm." I knew that I was making a big mess of things. There was so much in my heart that I wanted to say, but I couldn't tell if my words had any effect on her. She continued to watch me. She took everything in, not missing a beat.

"Then why have you come?"

"For my daughter. She ran across the bridge and into the pine forest. I tried to stop her, but she wouldn't listen to me. So, I went after her. I crossed the bridge. I looked for her everywhere, but I couldn't find her." My eyes began to fill with tears. "Then I followed the Akita, and he led me to the Eternal Night."

I wanted her to believe that I only did what a mother would do. I had to convince her. But that sadness began to overwhelm my heart. I couldn't help it. I missed him. When I thought about saying goodbye to him, the tears just wouldn't stop coming. In that moment, I hated myself for feeling that way, for not fighting for my daughter like her life, like my life depended on it. My heart was still with a ghost, and I didn't know how to get back to the living.

"But your daughter isn't the only reason you are here, am I correct?"

"Yes. But that wasn't my intention. When I crossed that bridge, all I was thinking about was my daughter."

"You have met the guardian of the Eternal Night?"

"Yes. I know that he is my husband who died three months ago. I didn't know that I would get to see him. Maybe in my heart I was always hoping. Is that so wrong?" She didn't answer me. She didn't try to understand. "He's the one who took me to see my mother. He's the one who told me that I needed to see you."

"Well, he's right, that is, if you desire to go back."

"I do. I know that I'm human, and this is not my place. I don't belong here. But if you let me go home, I will treasure the gifts you have given me for the rest of my life."

"Can you honestly live without Naoki? Can you move on?" I wanted to tell her the truth, that I couldn't, that I didn't want to leave this place, that I wanted to stay with him forever. But when I thought about my daughter, I swallowed my grief.

"I don't have a choice, do I?"

There was a long pause. The woman stood up, her kimono swishing against the wooden floor. Her movements were so graceful; for a moment there, I thought she was going to jump into the lake and turn into a magical koi. But she stopped at the edge of the veranda and looked out upon the lotus field.

"Sometimes, I like to sit here when I want to feel bright again. Do you know what I mean, Nami?" I met her gaze. *It couldn't be.* All at once, I saw her wearing that red apron, her hair pulled back from her face, those apple-colored cheeks and lips, and that basket in her hand, full of twilight blue hydrangeas.

"Akane? Is that you?"

THE WOMAN TURNED AROUND AND SMILED, her eyes twinkling in the moonlight. Before I knew it, she had knelt down in front of me and bowed low.

"I am Inari, the fox kami."

"It was you? You were the one at my father's house that day?" She nodded. My head was spinning now. "But I don't understand."

"Do you remember when you were a little girl and you used to sit in your father's garden at night? The moon loved to see your face. You shone so bright that even the night was no match for your heart."

I looked up at the moon in the land of the living. I saw its face, and all at once, I wanted to be in that light again. I wanted to feel that brightness. "I remember."

"But when your mother left, she took that light with her, and your father took what was left. If you couldn't make any light of your own, that was no way to raise a child, was it?" I nodded. In that moment, I felt so bad for my daughter. I had nothing to give her, no brightness to share. All this time, I had been stealing her light, until she, too, was left in the darkness.

"Is that what you meant when you said I was running out of time? That I would lose my daughter?"

"Yes. Since your mother left, the scales began tipping farther and farther to the night. And then, what your father did to you only pushed you deeper into that darkness. Of course, Naoki's death was the final blow. At that point, you couldn't recover. You were getting closer and closer to joining them on the other side, leaving your daughter to grow up by herself." In that moment, I couldn't meet her gaze. I knew she was right, that she spoke the truth. Inari was looking right at me now, but I couldn't face her.

"I haven't seen my daughter smile since Naoki died, and I haven't done anything about it. I just couldn't get past losing him. It was like so much had already been taken away from me. And then, when he died, it was beyond unfair. I just couldn't go on."

Inari took my hand in hers. Her hand was surprisingly cold, and her skin a snow white. "You made a wish when you were young to see your mother again. 'Even just once would be enough,' you said. I could not ignore a wish from such a good person."

I turned away from her then. "I'm not a good person. This whole time, all I've ever thought about was myself."

"That's not true. When your mother left, love still lived on inside of you. And you gave that love to my messenger, the white fox who visited you in the night. And no matter what your father or the villagers thought, a part of you never gave in to the thought that your mother was a fox. You tried so hard to believe in her to the very end."

"But even now, all I can think about is what I've lost. In the Eternal Night, I didn't once think about my daughter. A good mother wouldn't have done that. She would've put aside her own desires, her own losses for the good of her child."

"But you *are* a good mother. You have traveled to an unknown land. You have said goodbye to someone you deeply loved. You have done whatever it takes, no matter how painful. All for the sake of your daughter."

"No, I think all my heart cared about was Naoki. Now, all I'm left with is grief and guilt." In that moment, I could still feel Naoki's hand on my cheek, his voice in my ears, his lips on mine. My heart ached with such longing.

"I know."

"I miss him, Inari. So much so that I can't get through the day sometimes."

"He misses you too." I started sobbing. The pain of losing him again was just too much to endure. "But Naoki loved you more than you ever knew."

"Yes, I know. I know that he loved me. He told me how he's tried to find me in every lifetime, how I'm Kasumi, his one true love."

"While all of that is true, Nami, perhaps, it was his love for you in this lifetime that was the greatest of all."

"I don't understand."

"Do you know why Naoki was at the river the day he died?" I shook my head. There was so much I wanted to ask him, so much more I wanted to say, but we ran out of time. I didn't think it possible that he would leave me again. It seemed too painful to even consider. "That day, he was there to meet with your father."

"My father? Why would he do that?"

"About a year ago, he met your father by accident at the hospital. It wasn't that your husband felt sorry for him at all, but knowing that your father was dying made Naoki question what he used to believe. He knew you were still carrying around that darkness. Even though your father wasn't in your life anymore, he still lived on inside of you. He still had power over you. And Naoki didn't want that for you or for Suzu. So, before he died, he made a wish for you to find that brightness again, that light he knew still lived on inside of you."

"Is that why he wanted me to go see him?"

"Yes. Deep down, he wished for you to make peace with what happened to you."

"How did he die? Please, tell me. I need to know."

"He died, saving your father from killing himself."

"What? I don't understand."

"Your father was going to jump off that bridge, but Naoki saved him, like he saved you."

"Then why didn't my father come forward? Why didn't he tell me? Didn't he know that I was suffering?"

"He was scared. Fear makes people do bad things. And by that time, your father was too sick to do anything anyway." That anger was starting to build inside of me again. The irony of his death was not lost on me. Naoki died while saving the one person who ruined my life.

"I'll never forgive him! I'll never forgive my father!"

"But it's precisely that feeling that Naoki didn't want you to hold onto. Even when he arrived in the Eternal Night, he begged me to help you. And I cannot turn away from such a great love."

"But you know what my father did."

"I do. But I also know that your light is so much brighter than that. That is why you are here, that is why you got to see your mother again."

"Why did you let me see her?"

"Because now more than ever, you needed to see her. It was the only way you could be a true mother to your own daughter. You needed to remember what that love felt like, what a mother's love felt like."

"Why?"

"So that you could let go of the darkness. So that you could make your own daughter smile again. If you didn't move forward, neither would your daughter. And you remember what it was like to grow up without a mother, don't you?"

"But I don't want to move forward if it means letting go of that anger. It's all I have left of that time with my father. Just because he died, doesn't mean he gets to win. I just want to find my daughter now and go home."

"Your daughter is already waiting for you in Kasumi-machi."

"What? I have to see her then. You have to let me return to her."

Inari smiled gently. "Unfortunately, Nami, it's not that simple."

"What do you mean?"

"You are human, and you have seen a lot of things that you were not supposed to see."

"But I needed to see them, right? You said that I had to see my mother, that I needed to feel her love."

"If you want to return to the earthly plane, you must first be willing to give up your memories of this place."

"You mean, my mother? No, I want to remember her."

Inari shook her head. After all this time, we had been reunited. *How could I go on living without even the memory of her here?* The thought of having my time with her erased, made me feel that loss all over again. "You will not remember Naoki either — at least not the man you met in the Eternal Night."

"No!" I cried. I got down on my hands and knees and begged her to change her mind. "You can't do this! Haven't I suffered enough? I don't want to forget him. At least give me that." But she wasn't listening to me.

"Naoki has made his vow. He will always be protecting your heart. No matter where you go, he will be there, watching over you."

"But how will I move on if I don't remember?"

"You will always feel their love. Suzu will help you to remember them. Every time you see her face, you will think of Naoki and your mother. In every kindness you experience in your life, every brush of the wind on your cheek, every stream of sunlight on your skin holds their love. Then one day, when it is your time, you will return to Naoki again."

Her voice was so gentle. In that moment, Inari could have told me that I would never return to Kasumi-machi again, and I would have accepted it. Even now, the thought of leaving my mother behind in the Weeping Field and Naoki in the Eternal Night felt necessary when Inari said it. If this was what it took to go back, then I was going to do it. I needed to see Suzu again. I didn't want her to grow up like me with a heart too small to love anyone.

"Inari, I want to go back. I'm willing to do whatever it takes to return."

She smiled again and gently gazed down at her hands. "Giving up your memories is the easy part."

"I don't care," I told her. "Tell me what else I have to do."

- 27 -

INARI TOOK THE MOON FROM THE SKY and placed it in my heart. All at once, I was at my father's house again. Naoki was there. He was holding me close in the bright moonlight. I could feel his breath on my ear. He was whispering something to me. But no matter how hard I tried, I couldn't hear what he was saying. *Why couldn't I hear him?* I was so desperate now, that I couldn't see the darkness closing in around me. It began to fill my entire being, until soon, he was gone.

"Naoki!" I cried. "Naoki!" But he wouldn't answer me. "Naoki, come back! Please, Naoki. Tell me what you said." I kept calling to him. I kept hoping he would reappear in front of me. I didn't want him to end up just being a feeling in my heart. I wanted to see his face again. I wanted to memorize every last detail. The way he looked at me, the way he smiled. His laugh. All that I missed began to weigh heavy on my heart. I dropped down to the floor and buried my face in my hands.

"Naoki is with you," Inari whispered, "no matter the distance." I wanted to believe her. I wanted to believe that he'd always be there, but the darkness just felt so heavy, like it would never lift, like it would never allow me to see him again.

All of a sudden, I felt it, a tiny spark. Something inside of me was humming with joy. "Mama," she whispered. At the sound of her voice, tears filled my eyes. Even in my grief, my daughter had never given up. She was always searching for me, always trying to guide me home.

"Suzu."

"Mama, come back to me." I gently touched my heart. In that moment, I missed her so much, and that longing grew deeper and deeper, until it was echoing in my womb.

"No matter what happens, Nami, your daughter will know that she was a part of you and Naoki. She will know that she was loved. You can be assured of that." The way Inari said it, it was like my fate had already been decided.

"No! I need to go back!" I begged. "Please, Inari. I don't want Suzu to grow up alone." I got down on my hands and knees and bowed with all the reverence I had for the fox goddess. I didn't want her to make a decision just yet.

By the time I looked up again, the darkness had lifted, but Inari was gone. I stood up. My eyes searched all around me. I could still hear her voice, but the veranda was deserted. All that remained was me and the moonlight. But not for long. In the cool of the night, I saw the bridge, and a figure began to appear just beyond the other side. Moments later, what was once transparent had now become solid. And here, in the land of the living, Inari had done the impossible.

My voice caught in my throat. Of all people, I hadn't expected to see him, not like this. He was young again and handsome. That boyish innocence radiated from his heart. I didn't recognize him. Not this version.

"It can't be," I whispered to myself.

"He is the same man," Inari replied.

"Why is he here? I don't need to see him. He isn't a part of my life anymore."

"But you need your father now, more than you know."

"You're wrong."

"Nami, once a human has found her way into the Weeping Field, it is too difficult for her to return on her own. Only love, true love can bring you back."

"Don't you see? I had that with Naoki."

"But love is not something to withhold," she said.

"What do you mean?"

"You cannot choose to give it to one person and not another. You cannot go back with a heart that beats like that. Only a line of pure love will return you to the human realm."

"I don't understand. I have it with Naoki, Suzu, my mother, even Bachan. What more do I have to do to prove to you that I can love, that my heart has grown bigger?"

"But you do not have that love for everyone." It didn't matter how she said it. When I heard those words, I couldn't stop my grief and hatred from rising up inside of me again. "True love does not make distinctions or conditions, Nami."

"But you know what he did."

"I do. But like Naoki, I also know how much more you can love. Your heart is so strong now that you can forgive him. I know you can. You can love him again."

"I don't know if I can."

I studied the man before me. His face was so warm, so kind. He had opened his arms, ready to hold me against his heart. A part of me so desperately wanted to run to him, but I couldn't move. I wouldn't.

"Sanae!" he cried. Her name pierced my heart. Even through my tears, I could see my reflection on the surface of the lake. I still looked so much like her.

The full moon rippled across the water. But it wasn't beautiful anymore. Its light touched my face and all at once, I was in that room again. I could see him clearly. I could see what he was doing. The whole time, I stared at my mother's urn. I pretended that I could disappear just like she had.

"I'm Nami," I said to him. "Don't you remember? I'm your daughter, Nami." I stared at him. Even though he was young, his eyes were already tired. I could see it. They had been searching just like mine. They had grown weary looking across that bridge day after day. All they wanted now was to see my mother again.

"Your mother's disappearance broke him inside. He didn't know how to make his heart whole. But your father wasn't always this way."

The world of Inari faded away, and I was back at my father's house again. But I wasn't twenty anymore. I must've been maybe three or four years old. I waited on the veranda with my mother like a human sun, beaming with yellow boots, a yellow sun hat and a yellow t-shirt and shorts.

"Papa!" When my father finally saw me, his eyes lit up.

"Mama," he said to my mother. "We're going to the river."

"Have a good time." She waved and smiled. My father planted a kiss on her cheek, and my mother blushed.

Then, my father hoisted me in his arms.

"Let's go, Nami. The fish are waiting for us." I held onto him tight, and he carried me all the way down the slope to the water. We played in the small pools at the bend in the river. Even though it was very shallow there, and I could walk in the water with ease, my father never took his eyes off of me. He made sure that I was safe. All that time, he talked with me as if we were the only two people in the world. *Why don't I remember this?* I thought to myself.

I looked at the man standing in front of me again. The mist was swirling around him as if he had been turned into a kind of spirit. He was beginning to fade.

Inari called my name. "There's not much time." But I couldn't remember. The man didn't look anything like the one I saw at the house the other day. How old he had become! The hatred and grief he had held onto had just eaten away at his heart until there was nothing left, until there was no trace of the man who stood before me.

"It's not him," I told her. With a bouquet of yellow flowers in his hand, the man looked so boyish and young, so innocent that my heart didn't register his image.

"It is," Inari insisted. It couldn't be. The man in front of me still believed in true love. He still had hope. He had no idea how broken he would become. He didn't know what he would end up doing to me years from that time. In that moment, I didn't know what I wanted from this man. I didn't recognize him. If anything, I wanted the one I saw yesterday to appear before me. I wanted that man to tell me that he was sorry. I stood my ground. But all the while, Inari kept on insisting.

"I am not asking you to forget what happened or make it go away. It's not that simple. What he did was unforgiveable. But deep in your heart, your father's love for you is still there."

"I don't remember," I said to her. "No matter how hard I try, I just don't."

"Think back," Inari began, "think far back before he turned into a man you couldn't recognize." She spoke close to my ear in a whisper. "Try, Nami. Look deep into your heart. His love is there." I had wanted to all along, but how could I forgive someone like that? He had hurt me. He had betrayed me to my core. In that moment, I started to doubt if I would ever get to go back. I wanted to see Suzu again. I wanted to be with Bachan. But I couldn't remember. And as long as I couldn't remember, home was always going to be just out of my grasp.

I felt desperate. I was fighting with the darkness inside of me, but even now, I couldn't tell who was winning. Then, all of a sudden, I heard it—a slow whisper near my ear. "Live, Nami. Live as if you already have his love." I closed my eyes. I felt Naoki's love fill my entire being. I let it sink down deep into my heart, past the Weeping Field and the Eternal Night to the darkness, to the places I had shut away for too long. In that instant, I saw my father again. He was waiting for me at the edge of the bridge.

"Nami!" The man called out to me. "Nami! I'm sorry!" He kept repeating those words like a prayer, until it sank down deep into my soul. After a while, he disappeared. But I didn't need to see him anymore, because in his voice, I knew he had meant it.

After my mother disappeared, there wasn't a day that went by that I didn't dread going to school. My classmates were cruel. They called me fox daughter, even before the villagers began to talk behind my father's back, before he was a fool in their eyes.

But the worst days, where it was a sheer test of my willpower to go the whole time without crying, were when our mothers were invited to spend the day with us. I couldn't help but watch the other kids. I was hungry for love, for comfort as their mothers doted on them in front of me. I'd study their faces, every inch of their skin, wondering if my own mother's face was as bright with love when she looked at me. Time was cruel in that way. With the passing of each year, I was less and less sure if the face that I was remembering was really Mama's. Deep down, I was so afraid that I had already forgotten her.

That day, it was my teacher who helped me with my lunch and smiled at me, bright with love, just like all the other mothers in the room. For that one moment, I almost believed that she was my real mother, that I wasn't beyond love. I let myself be comforted by the fact that at least I had someone there with me.

Maybe my father could have come in my mother's place. Maybe he could have been the one to help me with my lunch and dote on me like all the other mothers. But after my mother disappeared, he drowned himself in his work. He must have been so terrified of his own sadness that he was going to run from it, until he couldn't run anymore, and eventually, it would kill him. He couldn't look at me, let alone spend any time with me without feeling that grief laced with resentment. I must have been a constant reminder to him of what he had lost. It didn't matter. My father was unskilled at being a mother anyway, that softness, that gentleness she had in this life, he could never duplicate.

But that one day, just as I was gazing into my teacher's face, my father showed up, unannounced.

"C'mon, Nami," he said. He had come with bento lunches and fishing gear. I was so surprised that I didn't know what to say. He smiled at me. He was young again like my mother. He wasn't angry yet. He was the Papa I remembered.

That day, he set an urn on the altar for Mama. Deep down, he didn't know if she had run away. He didn't know if she were coming back, or if she were even alive, but he didn't want me to remember her that way. It might have seemed strange to me then, but I realized that it was my father's way of loving me. He wanted me to remember her when she was here. He didn't want me to keep holding on, even though, in the end, he would be the one who couldn't let go.

We went down to the water, walking upstream, past the bend in the river. I couldn't see the bridge unless I really tried. Both of us knew it was there, but we didn't want to think about it. Instead, we spent our time along the banks, listening to the river and skipping stones across the water. We were there until the sun went down, and Papa had to carry me back to the house.

My father made rice balls and fried fish. It wasn't like my mother's, but I remembered how good it tasted. I let that memory fill my heart now. He was still trying to be my Papa then. He hadn't given up yet or let his grief overtake his life.

This Papa was warm and loving. My heart swelled. I felt my father's heart and his love for me. I knew then that if I held onto that memory, I could live again. I could live as though I already had his love.

And when I finally opened my eyes, I was standing at the edge of that pine forest.

- 28 -

THE FOREST LOOKED EXACTLY HOW I HAD LEFT IT. Only now, the morning sun broke through the fog, and the shadows didn't scare me anymore. I remembered what was on the other side of those trees. I thought about Kasumi-machi, the home of my mother and father, the place where I met Naoki for the first time, and where my daughter was waiting for me.

If I had my way, I would leap over this whole forest and land right at the edge of the bridge. I would run straight across, calling to her. And when Suzu was standing right in front of me, I would lift her up into my arms and hold her forever. I had no idea how long I had been gone or how long it had been for Suzu, but I hoped that she still believed in me. I hoped that she was still there.

Inari appeared at my side. She smiled at me, her eyes twinkling just as they did when I met her at my father's house.

"I know that you will not remember your time in the Weeping Field, nor your meetings with your mother or Naoki. It is such a large price to pay for a journey back to the human world. But someone like you, with such a good heart, should not leave here without a gift."

"You've already given me so much, Inari. After all this time, you let me see my mother again, and I got to see Naoki. You gave me the chance to say goodbye. That's more than enough to last a lifetime."

"And your father?"

"I think I understand now why Naoki wanted me to go see him. He knew my heart was so much bigger than what had happened to me. He knew that I could love so much more. But I didn't know that. And the only way I would is if I saw him again."

"Even just once would be enough." I couldn't help but tear up at the sound of his words.

"I'm sorry."

"Do not be sorry for loving someone. You love him and Naoki loves you. And that will never change."

When she said that, I couldn't hold back my tears. In that moment, I realized just how much I was leaving behind.

"Yes, I know it's going to be hard, but I'm ready now. You've already helped me to free my heart. Because of you, I can truly love my daughter again, like how she deserves. I think it's what Naoki always wanted for me and for her."

"It is."

"So that's more than enough for me."

"Still, I want to give you something anyway, so that you'll become aware of what you had been given a long time ago."

"Something I'd been given?"

"Yes." She took my hand in hers and held it open. In a few moments, an old photograph appeared in my palm as if she had pulled it out of thin air.

"For me?" Inari nodded. It was an old black and white photo. In it, there were two young women a little younger than me. The woman on the left wore a yukata with small flowers. Her hair was swept up, away from her face, and tucked into those beautiful black waves were two hair ornaments with tiny bells. In her hand, she held a lacquered umbrella behind her, which I knew could only be red. I smiled when I saw her. There was no doubt that this was my mother.

I didn't recognize the other woman at first. Dressed in a solid-colored kimono, her long black hair was gathered into a loose bun at the nape of her neck. But when I looked closer, I saw the gentleness in her eyes, a tender warmth that seemed to radiate from her heart. All at once, it dawned on me who it was. When I looked up, Inari was already smiling.

"They were the best of friends in her first life," she said. "She was with your mother at the bridge on the night that she died."

"She's Takako? Bachan is Takako?"

"Yes." I felt like such a fool. I should have known it was her. I don't know why I didn't make the connection.

"You couldn't have known," Inari said to me.

"Is that why she took me in?"

"She meant it when she told you that she wanted you to live with them. There was no hesitation."

"She did it for Mama."

"And for you, Nami." In that moment, I loved Bachan even more than she would ever know. When Naoki begged her to let me live with them, she could have said no, she could have turned me away. But she took me in, cared for me as if I were her own flesh and blood. She never knew my secret. She never knew what had happened with my father, but it didn't matter to her. She loved me anyway.

In my heart, I couldn't stop thanking Inari. She had given me such a wonderful gift. A treasure. I had been so blind. But now, I realized that love had been there all along.

It hadn't left me at all. Yes, there was pain. There was grief and unimaginable hurt. Some days I resented the whole world. But even on those days, I was never alone.

I vowed to be good to Bachan. I vowed that I would cherish the gift that Inari had given me. I smiled at her. My heart was so full of love.

"Thank you, Inari. Truly, thank you."

I looked down at the photo in my hand and smiled to myself. I had so much to tell Bachan when I got home. I knew the truth now. I knew what was real. She wouldn't have to feel guilty anymore. I was going to make sure of it. I wanted to thank Inari one more time. I wanted to say goodbye to her. But when I looked up again, she was gone. She had faded into the morning light.

I was alone at the edge of that pine forest, but I wasn't afraid.

"Goodbye, Inari," I whispered.

- 29 -

THE MORNING AIR WAS CRISP, ALMOST COLD, not anything like what summer should have been. But I welcomed the cold. It reminded me of the snow, and the stars falling from the sky. Once I left the shadow of the pines, and stepped onto that bridge, I wouldn't remember seeing my mother again. I wouldn't remember the Weeping Field. And the amber light that felt like home would become just a warm feeling in my heart that I couldn't explain.

"Naoki," I whispered. That gentle soul of my heart felt so close, as if the Eternal Night lived on inside of me. I wished more than anything that I would live a life that Naoki could be proud of, that maybe I could even fall in love again. I wanted to have a lifetime to tell him about when we met years from now. I felt his warmth on my skin, as if he were holding me in his arms. I looked up. The sun had broken through the canopy of trees. Standing in that stream of light, I felt his love fill my entire being. And I knew in my heart that somehow, he would always be a part of me. Under that blue sky, I was bathing in that brightness. I was shining again.

I closed my eyes. In the distance, I could hear the river. It wouldn't be long now. I let its voice fill my heart. I let it speak to me like it was an old friend. Standing there alone, held in that light, I felt at peace. It was as though this rare silence began to grow inside of me. And then, I heard it. It was small and faint at first. It was nothing that I had ever known before. A tiny voice, a cry, traveled through time and space until it finally reached me. I touched my womb.

From somewhere deep in my soul, I heard that small cry again. Tears ran down my cheeks, but these were happy tears. "Naoki. You knew, didn't you? You knew that I wasn't going to be alone. You were going to find a way to always be here with me, to watch over me, to protect me." I looked up at the sky, so blue like that day at the bridge. "Naoki. Thank you. Thank you, Naoki."

I stood in that summer sun just a little longer. I wanted to remember that warmth. I wanted to soak it in, so that every cell of my being felt it. I wanted it to become so indelible that even on the hard days, the days where I felt like I couldn't go on, I would remember how much I was loved. And I'd remember then that he hadn't left me at all.

When I walked away finally, I was filled with light. The sun and the blue sky were behind me, but I was shining. I was entering the last stretch of shadows, but even in the darkness, the forest didn't feel ominous anymore. It felt hopeful. Love could be sustained in that night. As I got closer and closer, I began to sense it, like someone was following me. Footsteps, soft and gentle fell on the forest floor. My heart raced. I knew it was impossible, but a part of me hoped it was true. He had to be here. I just wanted him to know. I wanted him to know he would be a father again.

But when I finally turned around, it was the Akita. He peered out from behind one of the pine trees. This time, I ran to him and buried my face in his thick white fur. If I had my way, I would never let go. But the Akita began to bark. And when I looked up again, beyond the trees, I saw the bridge. It gleamed in the sunlight, and all I wanted to do was run to it.

I looked back one last time. I couldn't see Inari's home anymore or the Weeping Field or even the Eternal Night, but I had to have faith that they were there, waiting for me. I had to believe they were thinking about me—Mama and Naoki—just as I was thinking about them. Deep down, I hoped Inari was right. I hoped that feeling, the love of those places and people would remain in my heart forever, even after my memory of them had faded.

"Goodbye," I whispered to the wind. I saw the bridge up ahead. The day was so bright that I wondered if this was still a dream. I ran toward the light. The yellow flowers were blooming across the river now. I couldn't wait to be in their warmth. And the sound of water was so loud. It filled my heart again until I could hear nothing else.

I could see her now. She was waiting on the other side of the bridge. My daughter was holding Bachan's hand. From where I stood, I watched as her eyes looked far across to the other side. She was looking for me, searching with those big eyes just as I had done so many years ago. I wanted to run to her. I wanted her to forget that I had ever been gone.

I turned back to the Akita. His eyes were so familiar now, so much like someone I had loved. My heart ached with everything I was leaving behind. But the pull of the light was too strong. I didn't hesitate. I ran from the pine forest, from the darkness I had carried inside of me for too long. The light was beckoning, and all I had to do was step into it. Once freed from the shadows, my daughter spotted me in an instant.

"Mama! Mama!" she cried. She ran toward me. Tears streamed down my cheeks. *How long had she waited?* I ran as hard as I could, but even now, I couldn't get to her fast enough. Then, all of sudden, she was in my arms. I held onto her like I would never let her go. And below us, the river rushed past, the one he had drowned in and the one he had saved me from.

How simple it would have been to die in that river! If Naoki hadn't saved me that day, none of this would have ever happened. I wouldn't have arrived at this age. I wouldn't have seen this day. I wouldn't have fallen in love with him or had his child. I wouldn't have had to say goodbye to him. If Naoki hadn't saved me, there would be no more pain, no more tears. He should have left me at the bottom of that river. I should have drowned that day.

But I lived.

Author's Note

Inari is one of the primary Shinto gods or *kami*. She is often known as the god of rice and prosperity, and she has a strong connection to foxes. You will see fox statues at Inari shrines like Fushimi Inari in Kyoto. While she has been represented in various forms, I have chosen to portray Inari as a benevolent female goddess, someone who can grant wishes. I have also incorporated her connection to foxes in the novel.

For more information on Inari, a good book to start with is *The Fox and the Jewel* by Karen A. Smyers.

Acknowledgements

When I was in graduate school, I had a teacher who once told me, "You're lucky. Stories seem to find you." I don't think I really believed her then, but after all this time with *The Weeping Field*, I'd have to agree. This novel found me. And in the process, it took me on such a journey in my own life, that I can't help but think that it might have been divinely inspired. (Maybe one day, I'll write a book on that.) No words can truly express how grateful I am to all the people who were a part of my journey. Still, I can't help but try.

I met Tetsuo and Keiko a decade ago, when I went to Japan for the first time by myself. They had never met me. They were friends of my parents. But they welcomed me with open arms and taught me so much about unconditional love. They were very instrumental in creating the location and atmosphere of the novel. We had many conversations about names, words, places, and characters. This novel would not be what it is without their input, and even now, I can feel their love and spirit woven through every word.

Eleven years is a long time. I don't remember how many times I threatened to throw this manuscript away. But my mom always encouraged me to wait, to shelve it for the moment, and try again later. And, of course, she told me that if I ever did throw it away, she would climb into that trash bin, even if it had cat crap, and rescue it. Every. Single. Time. Thank you for believing in this novel, Mom, and for always believing in me.

If he had his way, I know my father would have wanted me to choose a more stable job. But despite the fact that he doesn't always understand the path I've chosen nor does he always like the way I write—*too many flashbacks*—that's never stopped him from trying to find ways to show his support. Sometimes, I don't think I give him enough credit for how well he knows my heart. Thank you, Dad.

There are some friends that stick around for a season or a reason, but a few are there for practically a lifetime. I'm so lucky, Kim, that you are in my life. You have listened when others have turned a deaf ear. You have cheered me on and encouraged me, especially during the hard times. Can't wait till we're old, sitting on the porch, eating scones and talking about everything and nothing. Thank you also for reading the novel and giving such great feedback.

Sometimes you need to be seen. You need to be told the words that you needed to hear when you were young. Thank you, Bev, for seeing me and for telling me those words. You have always been there for me, and I am so blessed because of you.

Brandi, you read this novel first, back in the day. I am so grateful for your insight, kindness, and time all those years. I couldn't have gotten through it all without you. Thank you for the pink post-its on my desk reminding me of who I am.

Kazuko, I am so glad that we got a chance to spend time together on that first trip to Japan. I'll always remember how you told me that the kind of man I want doesn't exist. One day, you'll see that you were wrong. Ha ha! Thank you also for all of your advice and insights about the novel. I couldn't have done it without you.

Jake, I'm so grateful that you and Doug were in my life all those years. Thank you for your friendship. You were always there to lend an ear, and you never stopped believing that I could do this, that I could create this book. Thank you for believing in me, especially when I didn't believe in myself.

Abby, thank you for supporting me and my work for all these years. Even back in the day when you worked at the airline, you were always cheering me on.

Janis & Lloyd, thank you for popping into that stationery shop so long ago. When I told you that I left teaching to pursue writing, you said to me, "You're so brave." I have never forgotten your words. They continue to inspire me.

Thank you, Joan. You were the only other person who really encouraged me when I left teaching. Even though I felt so lost, you said to me—"Do you want to be one of the 99% of people who are doing the same thing for the rest of their lives or do you want to be that 1% that's living their dream? You know, that 1% are the people who get rich." Thank you for realizing then how much more difficult it would be to live with regret.

A big, big thank you to the early readers of my book who showed me that I was on the right path, and that I had created something worth reading.

Thank you, Galyn, for taking the time to read both the original version and the final version of the novel. Your feedback, encouragement and offerings of dessert really kept me going.

Thank you to the people who read this last version and gave me such great feedback: Denby, Ken, Maki, and Darold.

Big shout out to Jaime! Every writer needs a Jaime. Thank you for loving my work so much that you've written all over the manuscript, you've reread parts that are your favorite often, and you're so involved with my story that till the very end, you were holding out for the happy ending. Love you, girl!

Thank you to Glenn, Amy, Leilani, Noelani, Amanda, Dennis, and Brandon for being there, especially during the hard times.

Thank you to James, Blue and G. I wouldn't have come this far without the three of you.

Thank you, Dean, for looking at every single cover design I created and revised and giving such great feedback.

Thank you to Kathy, who really encouraged me to publish my novel when I was unsure if I really wanted to do it.

Thank you, Sandra, for long talks (that involved a lot of complaining) and to Keala for her continual support.

Thank you, Jen, for teaching me to celebrate myself and to trust in my own unique path.

Thank you, Julia for your steadfast encouragement always.

Thank you to Azra, Seren, Jade and the entire Biomancy team for a profound journey.

Thank you to all the people in Japan who helped me create this novel and dream new novels for the future, especially Yoko U., Katsuyo, Shigeo, Yoko T., Maya, and Bruno.

And to my readers, I hope this book in your hands really moves you in the way Nami's story and life moves me. I hope you will read this story again and again on the dark, overcast days of your life when you need a little light in that eternal night. Thank you, reader, for choosing my book, reading my words and hopefully, being moved by my story. I am forever grateful.

About the author

Mariko Miyake is an artist, writer, and lover of animals, real and imagined. She has been telling stories since her father used to take her for walks in her stroller. When she's not writing or painting, you can find her cooking, connecting with friends and family, and basically, letting her inner child lead the way. She hopes to have a dog one day. Until then, she'll have to create a whole pack of them in her dreams. *The Weeping Field* is her first novel.

To learn more, please visit: www.marikomiyake.com

The
Weeping
Field
a novel

m a r i k o m i y a k e

Sometimes you have to lose things in order for new things, people, answers, storylines, and even characters to come into your life. The more I travel on this creative life journey, the more I am amazed by the magic that comes with letting go.

Join me on my Substack account, *Otoshimono*, my own personal lost & found, where I write about the things I had forgotten, the things I want to remember and all the ways I've been found. Hope to see you there!

Subscribe: https://otoshimono.substack.com/